About the Book

Miss Pickerell will stop at nothing to prevent the closing of the Square Toe County Home for Retired and Disabled Animals. To get funds to save the Home, she agrees to be the star of the International Antique Car Fair in England. But disaster strikes when she, her cow Nancy Agatha, her middle nephew Euphus, and the Governor land in London. The Antique Car Fair parade has been called off because of an energy crisis.

Euphus's idea to use ethanol as a substitute fuel is a solution worth fighting for. Miss Pickerell goes into action!

Her thirteenth adventure sees her besieging the American Embassy, making a fiery speech in the British Parliament, and crossing the rough English Channel in an ancient helium balloon. As usual, Miss Pickerell's fans can count on her to come through.

Miss Pickerell Tackles the Energy Crisis

GAS
SORRY NO GAS
PUTT PUTT

Miss Pickerell Tackles the Energy Crisis

ELLEN MACGREGOR and DORA PANTELL
Illustrated by CHARLES GEER

McGRAW-HILL BOOK COMPANY
NEW YORK • ST. LOUIS • SAN FRANCISCO • AUCKLAND • BOGOTÁ • DÜSSELDORF • JOHANNESBURG • LONDON • MADRID • MEXICO • MONTREAL • NEW DELHI • PANAMA • PARIS • SÃO PAULO • SINGAPORE • SYDNEY • TOKYO • TORONTO

FOR CARRIE AND JENNIE,

MY DELIGHTFUL YOUNG FRIENDS,

WHO WILL NEVER OUTGROW MISS PICKERELL

Library of Congress Cataloging in Publication Data

MacGregor, Ellen.
Miss Pickerell tackles the energy crisis.

SUMMARY: When the antique car fair parade is called off because of the energy crisis, Miss Pickerell campaigns vigorously for the use of a fuel substitute thought up by her nephew.
[1. Fuel—Fiction. 2. Energy conservation—Fiction] I. Pantell, Dora F., joint author. II. Geer, Charles. III. Title.
PZ7.M1698Mpf [Fic] 79-24149
ISBN 0-07-044589-3

123456789 MUMU 876543210

Contents

DOOM

1
The Last Straw

Miss Pickerell pushed her new, oversized eyeglasses a little farther down on her nose and peered out over them to scrutinize the clock in the middle of the library wall. She checked the time, exactly 3:30 P.M., with the hands on her own wristwatch. Then she tucked two loose hairpins firmly into place under her black felt hat, took a thick pencil out of her knitting bag, and rapped briskly on the table in front of her.

"As chairlady of the Square Toe County Volunteer Council," she announced to the members seated around the table, "I am calling this meeting to order. Mr. Sweeney, our excellent off-duty fireman, has kindly consented to write down the minutes. He is taking the place of Miss Lemon, our regular secretary, who cannot be with us today."

Mr. Sweeney, seated at the far end of the table, looked up in embarrassment.

"I . . . I told you, Miss Pickerell," he said

anxiously. "I never studied shorthand. Of course, I'll write as fast as I can. . . ."

Miss Pickerell gave him an encouraging nod.

"And now to the business at hand," she went on. "Mrs. Pickett has agreed to postpone her report about our recent cake and plant sale to the next meeting. This afternoon we will talk only about the energy crisis. I see that Mrs. Broadribb has something to say."

"I certainly do," Mrs. Broadribb called out from her place between Mr. Sweeney and Mrs. Pickett. "I want to say most emphatically that it's about time the Square Toe County Volunteer Council did something to solve the energy crisis."

Professor Humwhistel, sitting alongside of Miss Pickerell to her right, pushed his unlit pipe from one corner of his mouth to the other. He loosened the top button of his high, old-fashioned vest and coughed twice.

"Just what did you have in mind, Mrs. Broadribb?" he asked.

Mrs. Broadribb did not answer him directly. She leaned diagonally across the table to address her remarks to the lady assistant sheriff, seated on Miss Pickerell's left. Both the assistant sheriff and Miss Pickerell looked uneasily at the bird-watching glasses that dangled from a cord around Mrs. Broadribb's neck. They kept bouncing up and down on her large bosom and they banged against the table with every excited breath that she took.

"I want to go on record," she said, her eyes fixed on the assistant sheriff, "as being definitely against the reduction of power in the traffic light at the corner of Main and Bloomsberry Streets. I protest that action to the representative of the law who is present at this meeting."

"I had nothing to do with the decision to dim those lights," Assistant Sheriff Swiftlee retorted icily. "I do not make the laws or regulations about energy conservation. I carry them out. And talking about laws brings up another subject. The litter baskets in front of the bank have disappeared again."

Mrs. Broadribb leaned back and smiled.

"Well," she said, "now, at least, you can sympathize with me, Assistant Sheriff Swiftlee. You showed very little feeling and certainly made no serious effort to apprehend the criminal when my second-best pair of bird-watching glasses was stolen. You wasted my time with all sorts of questions and—"

The squeaking of the outside door interrupted whatever else Mrs. Broadribb was going to say. Mr. Rugby, owner of the Square Toe County Diner, Moonburgers Our Specialty, entered. He was still wearing his starched chef's hat and long white apron and he panted heavily.

"I got here as fast as I could," he whispered, as he lowered himself into a chair facing Mr. Esticott, Square Toe City's chief train conductor, and Mr. Kettelson, the hardware store man. "My assistant came late. He—"

"Help is very difficult these days," Mr. Kettelson stated immediately. "Difficult and irresponsible. When I give up my business, it will be because of the poor help. There is, of course, also the matter of taxes and the fact that—"

Miss Pickerell stood up.

"You are getting off the subject, Mr. Kettelson," she said loudly to make herself heard above Mr. Kettelson's outburst. "As you very well know, we are here to discuss the energy crisis."

"They are related subjects," Mr. Kettelson, raising his voice still higher so that he could drown her out, insisted. "The price of oil makes manufacturing prices go up and the storekeeper has to charge more and customers don't have that kind of money. Why, practically nobody has come in to look at my new line of double-coated aluminum frying pans. I've even put them on sale at a loss to myself. But . . ."

"There's no money for anything," Mrs. Pickett sighed. "The garbage collections in Square Toe City have been cut down to—"

"And the potholes!" Mr. Sweeney, looking up from his notebook for a second, called out. "What about the potholes?"

"And the colossal nerve of the electric company!" Mrs. Broadribb burst out. "Plus the mistakes on the bills! I'm still waiting for a refund of seventy-six cents on my January bill. That was three months ago, but—"

"Myself," Mr. Esticott broke in, "I don't see why a country that has been able to launch a journey to Mars and send people to the moon can't solve a simple energy crisis. I also don't see why people don't use the trains more. We've reupholstered the seats, put clean doilies on the headrests, and even fixed the defective whistles. You'd think that . . ."

Miss Pickerell stopped listening. She picked up the umbrella and knitting bag she had leaned up against the table, put on the sweater that she had draped around the back of the chair, and patted her hat to make sure it was on straight.

"I'm leaving," she said. "My cow and my cat have been waiting outside in the trailer long enough. And I have my seven nephews and nieces to think about. They're coming to stay with me on the farm while their house is being painted. Why their parents decided to have the painting done during the school spring vacation, I'll never understand. But that's neither here nor there. I have a lot to do. And it isn't as though this meeting is—"

Professor Humwhistel coughed again.

"Yes, Professor?" Miss Pickerell asked. "Did you want to say something?"

"I have heard," Professor Humwhistel replied, "that your middle nephew, Euphus, has been collecting some interesting science information about solutions to our energy crisis."

Miss Pickerell smiled. She felt very proud of her middle nephew, Euphus. He talked too much and he was always arguing with his sister, Rosemary, but he was very good in science. She was just sitting down and trying to recall some of the things he had explained to her when Mrs. Broadribb raised her hand.

"I wish," she said, "that Professor Humwhistel would tell us a little something about what science has in store for us. In regard to the energy crisis, that is."

Professor Humwhistel studied his unlit pipe and looked very thoughtful.

"Well," he said, "there's nuclear energy."

"Never!" Miss Pickerell shouted. "With all those accidents and that dangerous radiation exposure! I wouldn't dream of it."

"Never! Never! Never!" Mr. Rugby echoed.

"I wasn't really thinking of nuclear fission," Professor Humwhistel apologized. "That comes from splitting the atom apart. I had in mind nuclear fusion, which is a joining of the atoms. I must admit, however, that the idea is still being

researched. I doubt that we can expect much from it in the very near future."

"Coal, then!" Mr. Rugby called out. "Good, old-time coal!"

Professor Humwhistel shook his head.

"We don't have enough coal to last more than a hundred years or so," he said. "There's also the danger of polluting the atmosphere. And long-term use of coal can lead to changes in the global climate, irreversible changes that—"

"I agree with Professor Humwhistel," Mr. Esticott interrupted. "I don't know what he means about those irreversible changes. But I do know that we no longer use coal on our trains and we are very satisfied."

Professor Humwhistel began to light his pipe with a match that he took out of his vest pocket. Then he saw the NO SMOKING sign and put his pipe away.

"I still haven't mentioned solar energy," he said. "The sun may be our one hope for eventually meeting our global energy needs. There are still economic and research problems. They may all be solved, although I cannot say exactly when."

"*May* is not enough in my work," Assistant Sheriff Swiftlee commented. "The important requirement is proof."

"PROOF!" Mrs. Broadribb shrieked. "That's what you kept saying to me when I named, actually *named* the person I suspected of stealing my bird-watching glasses. Proof, indeed!"

"I would also like Professor Humwhistel to tell us," Assistant Sheriff Swiftlee, throwing Mrs. Broadribb a cold glance, went on, "I would like him to tell us when he believes we can *expect* to be able to depend on the sun for our energy."

Mr. Sweeney, still writing at the end of the table, suddenly applauded. Mr. Rugby joined in the applause.

"Now, that's what I call a good question," he said.

Professor Humwhistel started to cough and changed his mind. He cleared his throat instead.

"It is certainly possible," he replied, "that we will be able to draw approximately seventy-five percent of the energy we need by sometime in the twenty-first century, perhaps the year 2035."

Mr. Kettelson laughed out loud.

"That's not going to bring my customers in," he said. "Or lower Mrs. Broadribb's electric bills."

Mrs. Broadribb nodded her agreement. Nobody said a word. Miss Pickerell looked around at the hopeless faces.

"I wish I could remember *exactly* what my middle nephew, Euphus, told me about a new science idea," she said. "It had to do with converting waste and surplus agricultural products into fuel alcohol for automobiles. Euphus even mentioned using plain garbage, I think, and . . ."

"Just the kind of nonsense a boy of his age would pick up!" Mrs. Broadribb snorted.

"Not at all!" Miss Pickerell snapped. "I have less than half a gallon of gas in my tank right now and with prices going up and supplies going down, I don't know when I'll get any more. Personally, I don't find the idea of using a substitute fuel the least bit nonsensical!"

She turned to Professor Humwhistel for his opinion. But the professor was absently tapping on the library table with the end of his gold-point pen and did not seem inclined to say anything. Miss Pickerell stood up again.

"If there is no further business," she announced, "I will hear a motion from the floor for adjournment of this meeting. Yes, Assistant Sheriff Swiftlee?"

"Not a motion," the assistant sheriff said. "A news item. The Home for Retired and Disabled Animals that this Volunteer Council worked so hard to establish last year is being shut down. For lack of funds."

Miss Pickerell nearly fell back into her chair.

"Impossible!" she exclaimed breathlessly. "The Home for Retired and Disabled Animals has a government grant of $25,000. I sent forty-nine letters myself to help get that grant!"

"The grant has to be matched by an equal amount in contributions," the assistant sheriff sighed. "I'm afraid the money is just not coming in. With the high prices of inflation, I suppose people don't have enough money—"

"I was explaining about all that," Mr. Ketelson broke in. "I was explaining about it exactly."

"And doing it very well," Mr. Esticott commented.

"He certainly did, didn't he, Miss Pickerell?" Mr. Rugby added.

Miss Pickerell did not answer him.

"This," she whispered, thinking desperately of all the poor animals who would now lose the only place they could call home, "this *is* the last straw!"

2
Miss Pickerell Makes a Deal

All the way back to the farm, Miss Pickerell kept thinking about the Home for Retired and Disabled Animals. What would happen to Homer, the deaf old plow horse who also suffered from rheumatism on rainy days? Homer could practically talk. He was always thanking everybody with his eyes for the loving care he was getting after all his years of hard labor. And what about Barney, the freckle-faced dog who had lost a leg under a runaway truck? Barney sat with Homer at mealtimes to make sure that no one disturbed him while he munched his ration of oats. And there was Emily, the cat whose owners had left her crying before an empty house when they moved away. Old Emily could no longer have children herself but she mothered every new animal that came into the Home, usually starting with a good face wash. And there were all the others—Ollie and

Rufus and Max and Pepper and Celia and Candy and . . .

"I simply can't adopt one hundred and ninety-eight animals," Miss Pickerell murmured to Pumpkins, her own big, black cat who sat purring on her lap while she drove. "And I *can't* let them die."

She blinked back the tears that were beginning to sting her eyelids and looked in the rear-view mirror to make certain that Nancy Agatha, her cow, was resting comfortably in the trailer. The trailer had a little, red-fringed awning over it to protect Nancy Agatha from bad weather. Miss Pickerell always took her cow and her cat along when she went out in her automobile. They loved the ride and she enjoyed their company.

"Those poor animals in the Home don't *want* to die," she went on, still talking to Pumpkins. "I *know*. I've seen how happy they are when they take a rest in the sunshine or when they feel the wind and smell the freshness of the flowers in the springtime. I *have* to do *something* to help them. I . . ."

The insistent honking of a number of horns behind her broke in on Miss Pickerell's thoughts. She steered her automobile over to the right-hand lane.

"I've never yet driven faster than thirty-five

miles an hour," she muttered, "and I don't intend to start now. What's more, *nobody* should be driving very fast when we're supposed to be conserving our oil."

She scowled as she watched three long, shiny cars and a baker's delivery wagon whiz by her and go roaring up the road. Pumpkins meowed his protest about the noise they were making.

"We'll be home soon," Miss Pickerell told him. "We can almost see the filling station from here."

At the filling station, Miss Pickerell took a horrified look at the new gasoline prices posted on the signboard and waved weakly when one of the attendants called out, "Hi, Miss Pickerell! Hi, Nancy Agatha! Hi, Pumpkins!" Then she carefully made the turn that took her off the highway and onto the private road leading up to her farm. She let out a sigh when she reached the top of the road and saw that Euphus and Rosemary had already arrived.

"And the other five will probably come tomorrow," she murmured. "I can only hope they don't talk me into a nervous breakdown."

Euphus and Rosemary were already busy talking, she noticed, as she came closer. They were carrying on an excited conversation with a stocky young man who was sitting on a very new motorcycle just outside the farmyard gate.

He had pale blond hair and he wore a bright red, polka-dot bow tie. Miss Pickerell knew who *he* was the minute she got out of her car and saw the bulging briefcase standing next to his motorcycle. She also knew that she had no intention of getting involved with a door-to-door salesman this afternoon.

"I have too much on my mind to think about magazine subscriptions," she said to herself, as she led Nancy Agatha out of her trailer and up toward the pasture. "And if it's those stylish new food processors he's selling, I'm personally not interested. I've said as much to Mr. Esticott, too."

Euphus, Rosemary, and the young man with the polka-dot bow tie were still talking when Miss Pickerell returned from the pasture. They had moved inside the gate and were standing near the freshly planted cucumber patch. The young man was holding a large manila envelope in his hand. Miss Pickerell had a good idea of what was probably inside.

"I have no time to look at your samples or your price lists today," she called out as she walked briskly in the direction of the wooden steps that led up to her kitchen. "I have other things to do."

Euphus and Rosemary ran after her.

"He's no salesman," Euphus shouted.

"He's Mr. Anthony Piffle, the American agent for the International Antique Car Fair," Rosemary said.

Mr. Piffle raced over to shake her hand.

"I'm very happy to meet you, Miss Pickerell," he said. "I can't begin to tell you how relieved I am to see that you look exactly like your picture. Mr. Cyril Chuff-Cooper, our representative in England, will be able to go full steam ahead now."

Miss Pickerell stared at Mr. Piffle. He didn't make much sense to her. But then almost nothing today had made very much sense.

"We'd better go inside," she sighed. "I'll talk to you as soon as I've fed my cat."

She filled Pumpkins' bowl and placed it on the mat marked CAT CAFETERIA even before she put her knitting bag and umbrella away. She did not bother to take off her hat.

"Now then, Mr. Piffle," she asked, "what *are* you talking about?"

Mr. Piffle answered by handing her the manila envelope.

"The picture's inside," he commented briefly.

Miss Pickerell opened the envelope and drew out a newspaper clipping that was pasted on cardboard and carefully covered on both sides with plastic. A large photograph took up most of the space in the clipping. It was a photograph of her, wearing the same black felt hat she had on today and sitting up very erect in her automobile. Nancy Agatha, her fawn-colored coat shining and her silver bell dangling around her neck, stood equally erect in the trailer.

"That's . . . that's the picture the newspapers took years ago, the day after I came back from the moon," she spluttered, "the time when the Governor got all those reporters together and . . . Where did you get this picture, Mr. Piffle?"

Mr. Piffle turned to Euphus. Euphus hung his head.

"I sent it," he mumbled, without lifting his eyes.

Miss Pickerell swallowed twice, while she waited for Euphus to continue.

"I saw this ad in *The Square Toe Gazette,*" he said finally, talking very fast. "It was about how they were looking for somebody for the Antique Car Fair and I—"

"That's right," Mr. Piffle interrupted. "We advertised *everywhere.* But it wasn't until we received your picture that we knew we had found what we wanted."

Miss Pickerell sat down in the nearest chair. She took a very deep breath.

"And what is it exactly that you *do* want?" she asked. "From me, that is?"

"Not very much, really," Mr. Piffle replied, taking the picture out of her hand and gazing at it happily. "We want you to fly to London with your old automobile and your cow and help us with the publicity for the International Antique Car Fair."

"The publicity for the International Antique Car Fair," Miss Pickerell repeated almost automatically because she was not at all sure that she had heard right.

"Yes," Mr. Piffle told her. "You'll drive your car with your cow in the trailer at the head of a parade through the streets of London and then through the surrounding countryside and on to Sussex Downs, on the coast, where the Fair is to be held. Everybody will be watching, of course, and—"

"Tell her about the other part!" Euphus burst out.

"The movie part! The movie part!" Rosemary shouted.

"I was coming to that," Mr. Piffle said. "We are filming the ride all along the route to Sussex Downs. That will be part of a movie scheduled for showing on worldwide television. You will be our star, Miss Pickerell, our star on worldwide satellite television."

He reached into his pocket for a handkerchief, shook it out, and mopped his brow. Miss

Pickerell noticed that the handkerchief had his initials embroidered on a corner.

"It is exciting, isn't it?" he exclaimed.

"And I can go, too!" Euphus screeched, jumping up and down and frightening Pumpkins off the windowsill where he had gone to take a nap after his supper. "Mr. Piffle said I could."

Mr. Piffle shrugged his shoulders.

"Your nephew insists that he is entitled to the trip as his commission for sending in the photograph," he explained. "It doesn't make much difference to us. We have chartered a plane. It will be a large cargo plane that can accommodate your car and your cow. And we have wired the British Ministry of Agriculture, Fisheries, and Food in Surrey for permission to admit your cow. It has to be *very special* permission because—"

Miss Pickerell had heard enough.

"Young man," she said icily, "I—"

"As I was about to say," Mr. Piffle continued, "we have also wired Washington for emergency passports and—"

"Young man," Miss Pickerell said again, standing up and walking over to look straight at him. "You'd much better stop talking and listen to me. I would not for one moment think of taking my cow and my car by cargo plane to

London or any other place. I would not dream of parading up and down highways and byways with Nancy Agatha to publicize a car fair. And as far as appearing in a movie on worldwide television is concerned, I can only say that it's the most ridiculous nonsense I have ever heard!"

"It's a two-hour movie," Mr. Piffle, who was not listening very hard, said proudly. "Not counting the commercials."

Miss Pickerell shuddered. If there was anything she despised, it was those endless commercials on television. But that was beside the point. She wished Mr. Piffle would go away. She wanted to go upstairs and think about a way to save the Home for Retired and Disabled Animals. She wondered if she ought to call the Governor. He would probably tell her that his budget was very tight. He was always saying that in his radio interviews. Miss Pickerell usually liked to listen to the Governor on the radio. Sometimes he talked on and on, though, the way Mr. Piffle was doing.

"We know," he was saying now, "that the trip may mean a sacrifice on your part. You will be away from your farm, which, according to this newspaper article, you love very much. And you will have to leave Pumpkins behind, though only for a few days. Animals entering England have to be quarantined. I *don't* think I can convince the British Ministry of Agriculture, Fisheries, and Food to make an exception of your cat. But we are prepared to pay you for your sacrifice, Miss Pickerell. We are prepared to pay the amount of—now, let me just see and make certain."

He took a piece of paper with a list of figures on it out of another pocket. He sat down at the table so that he could examine the figures carefully. Miss Pickerell left him to his calculations. She started walking over to her refrigerator to see what she could give Euphus and Rosemary for their supper.

"In American money," Mr. Piffle called after her almost immediately, "and at the present rate of exchange, it comes to approximately $20,000. The traveling expenses will be met in advance. The sum of $20,000, which represents the fee for your services, is payable upon completion of the two-day ride to Sussex and the one day spent at the Fair in Sussex."

Miss Pickerell wheeled around. This time she was *certain* that she had not heard right. Nobody in his or her right mind paid that kind of money for anything. In Square Toe County nobody even talked about such an amount. Peo-

STARDOM
$
FAME

ple read about it in newspapers and magazines but that was another world. That . . .

She was standing stock still in the middle of her kitchen when Mr. Piffle got up and waved the piece of paper in front of her.

"This is the conversion table," he said. "It converts British sterling into American dollars. You can see the figures for yourself."

Miss Pickerell walked back to her chair and sat down. Mr. Piffle was actually *serious!* He was offering her $20,000! $20,000! Why that . . . that was nearly as much as the Home for Retired and Disabled Animals needed to stay open. Nearly, but not *really* enough. She looked hard and long at Mr. Piffle, while idea after idea went round and round in her head. The only one that was any good was *completely* ridiculous. But she was going to try it. She *had* to . . .

"I . . ." she began.

Mr. Piffle waited. So did Euphus and Rosemary. She could almost hear the two of them holding their breath. She drew in a deep breath herself and stood up to face Mr. Piffle.

"Make it $25,000," she said, "plus traveling expenses, Mr. Piffle, and . . . and we leave tomorrow."

Mr. Piffle looked again both at the newspaper clipping and at Miss Pickerell. He looked again and again. Then he smiled broadly.

"If you promise, Scout's honor, Miss Pickerell," he said, "not to change your hat, I think we can call it a deal."

3
Off on a Cargo Plane

Mr. Anthony Piffle appeared on the nine o'clock local news broadcast the very next morning. He announced that Miss Pickerell and her cow were flying by cargo plane to London to take part in the International Antique Car Fair. Miss Pickerell's kitchen telephone rang two minutes later. It was the Governor calling to tell her that he was making arrangements to go with her.

"It will be good publicity," he said. "It will put our state on the map."

The Governor, Miss Pickerell reflected, was always saying something about putting a state on the map. Sometimes, when he made a public speech, he mentioned a number of states that he wanted to put there. Mrs. Broadribb often commented that she thought the Governor was planning to run for President. Mr. Kettelson, who telephoned after the Governor hung up, said almost the same thing.

"But that's not what I'm calling about," he went on. "I was wondering whether you might like me to stay on the farm with Pumpkins while you're away. Your mind will probably be at ease, if you know that I am with him."

Miss Pickerell couldn't agree more. There was nobody she knew, except maybe her veterinarian, who loved animals as much as Mr. Kettelson.

"I'm afraid there's a problem, however," she said, after she thanked him. "My nephews and nieces will be living on the farm while their own house is being painted."

"They'll be no problem to *me,*" Mr. Kettelson replied. "I can handle them."

He laughed out loud. So did Euphus and Rosemary, who were standing as close as they could to the telephone, listening to every word. Miss Pickerell did not have a chance to talk to them about this. Both her front and back doorbells were ringing.

Her sister-in-law, who was Euphus's and Rosemary's mother, came in the back way. She walked into the kitchen, carrying Euphus's duffel bag.

"He called me last night," she sighed, "after you'd gone up to bed. I didn't have the heart to say no to him. And now that I'm here, I'm going to help you pack."

"I don't need very much," Miss Pickerell told her. "Mr. Piffle wants me to look exactly the way I did in the picture."

"Nonsense!" her sister-in-law replied. "You may want to go somewhere special in the evening."

Rosemary nodded. She shared her mother's opinion.

"You certainly can't go anywhere in your skirt and your sweater and your old hat," she insisted.

She put Miss Pickerell's two best dresses and a pair of patent leather shoes into the suitcase when Miss Pickerell wasn't looking. Miss Pickerell was too busy letting in all the people who came to wish her a good journey and to bring her going-away gifts.

"But I'm only going for a few days," Miss Pickerell told them.

"What's the difference?" Mr. Sweeney asked, handing her a very fat book that was bound in green leather and had the word DIARY printed on the front. Miss Pickerell observed when she opened it that he had neatly printed the minutes of yesterday's library meeting on the first two pages.

"The way I figure it," he explained, "the meetings of the Square Toe County Volunteer

Council are an important part of your life and belong in your diary."

Mr. Sweeney had to go back to his fire station. But Mr. Rugby, Mr. Kettelson, Mr. Esticott, Professor Humwhistel, Mrs. Pickett, and Mrs. Broadribb stayed on. Mrs. Broadribb announced that she was making Miss Pickerell a present of her second-best bird-watching glasses. She had found them in a corner of her garden earlier that morning.

"I'm sure they were *returned,*" she said, as she hung the glasses around Miss Pickerell's neck. "And I know you will be glad to have them. I understand that the birds in England are especially interesting."

Miss Pickerell was trying to remember which birds flew mostly in England when the front doorbell rang again. Euphus raced through the parlor to see who it was. He returned with a panting Mr. Piffle.

"Good morning, all," he said. "Good morning, Miss Pickerell. You will be glad to hear that everything is under control. Here are your passports, some English money for small expenses, a signed certificate from your veterinarian, stating that Nancy Agatha has had all her injections and is in good health, *plus* the special permit allowing your cow to enter Britain.

You've no idea what I went through to get *that!* I talked long distance to the Ministry of Agriculture, Fisheries, and Food until I was almost blue in the face yesterday. I spoke about how important the Fair was for the British economy and . . ."

He paused a moment for breath. He went on while he was still inhaling.

"The permit was delivered by diplomatic pouch just a few minutes ago," he added. "There are special conditions attached. To prevent possible communication of disease, your cow cannot go near *any* other animal."

Miss Pickerell was getting ready to tell him what she thought of these doubts about her cow's *perfect* health, but she did not get a chance. Mr. Piffle was still talking.

"Mr. Cyril Chuff-Cooper who, as you know, Miss Pickerell, is our London managing agent," he said, talking very fast, "will be at the Heathrow Airport to greet you, to take you to your hotel, and to give you all the details about when and where the parade will start. The Governor is meeting us, with his passport, which doesn't need renewal, at Little Ridge. We board the cargo plane at Little Ridge. I can see by your face, Miss Pickerell, that you know it is a two-hour drive from here. We will start now."

Before Miss Pickerell even knew what was happening, Mr. Piffle had sent Mr. Kettelson to fetch the cow, carried Euphus's duffel bag and her umbrella, knitting bag, and valise out to the automobile, and was ushering her into the driver's seat and Euphus into the seat alongside her.

"Not before I explain to Pumpkins," Miss Pickerell protested, squirming out from under his firm grip on her right arm. "I have to find him."

"He's right here," Rosemary told her. "He's trying to get into the automobile with you."

Miss Pickerell picked Pumpkins up and kissed him gently.

"I won't be away long," she told him. "I have to go so that I can help those other animals in the Home. But Mr. Kettelson will take good care of you. And I'll telephone every night to hear how you're getting along. All right, Pumpkins?"

Pumpkins meowed only a little when Miss Pickerell handed him to Mr. Kettelson.

"He knows I love him," Mr. Kettelson said proudly.

"I love you all!" Mr. Piffle exclaimed. "But we have to get moving. I'm glad to see that you are wearing your sensible hat and shoes, Miss Pickerell. And I'm happy to note that Nancy

Agatha has her silver bell on. Now, you be sure, Miss Pickerell, that she wears it when they do the filming. It will add something to the picture and . . ."

He chattered all the way to Little Ridge, moving up on his motorcycle to her side of the automobile when there was no traffic on the road and tapping for her to roll down the window so that she would be able to hear him. Euphus, who also had a lot to say, kept leaning over and shouting to him. Miss Pickerell finally asked Euphus to climb into the trailer and continue his conversation from there. Euphus said it didn't pay. They would be at Little Ridge in less than five minutes.

"Oh!" he screamed a minute later. "There's the plane! She's super! Absolutely *super!!!*"

To Miss Pickerell, the cargo plane didn't look particularly exciting. It was big and it stood alone in a deserted airfield that, she decided, must once have been a farmer's pasture. It was also covered with thick layers of grime.

"Someone should take the trouble to remove that dirt," she commented to Mr. Piffle. "A good hosing down with some hot, soapy water is what it needs. Maybe a little ammonia added to the water for the rough spots . . ."

"The Governor? Where's the Governor?" Mr. Piffle shouted. "He has all my messages for Mr.

Chuff-Cooper, my last-minute publicity ideas. We discussed them over the telephone this morning. I called London to say he was bringing them, with all the details that I asked the Governor to write down."

Miss Pickerell couldn't care less. She was busy talking to the two cargo attendants who were directing her to a long ramp and she was telling Euphus to sit still, for heaven's sake, while she was also showing her passport and Euphus's to someone who asked for them.

"You can drive in this way," the cargo men told her. "Then you can move up to sit in the front seats of the plane."

"I'll do no such thing," Miss Pickerell retorted. "I intend to sit near my cow."

She drove cautiously up the wooden planks that looked to her as dirty as the rest of the plane. She had just reached the top and was entering the plane and turning her ignition off when she heard the Governor's booming voice.

"And I fully intend," he was saying, "to put Square Toe County and our state on the map."

He was standing up in the back of his long black limousine, surrounded by newspaper reporters and photographers. They took both notes and pictures, while he waved his passport in the air and continued to talk.

"Yes," he said, "I definitely believe in international cooperation. That is why I am accompanying Miss Pickerell, her nephew, and her cow on this trip. Nobody will ever say that I was too busy to do my bit for a program that can mean better relationships among the nations of the world."

He signaled to his chauffeur, who opened the door and escorted him out. He walked slowly up the ramp, twirling his cane and swinging the shiny leather case that he held in his other hand. He nearly bumped into Nancy Agatha's trailer when he turned around to take off his

top hat and call goodbye. Miss Pickerell got out of the automobile immediately to make sure that her cow was not alarmed.

"Miss Pickerell! Miss Pickerell!" the newspaper people shouted when they saw her.

Miss Pickerell moved back quickly. A whistle blew from somewhere in the field. The two attendants removed the wooden ramp. The door closed automatically. The whining of the starting engines drowned out the shouts of the reporters. Wheels turned as the heavy cargo plane began first its ride across the field and then its steady ascent.

"We're off!" Euphus screamed. "We're off!"

The plane, gathering speed, continued to climb. Mr. Piffle, on his very new motorcycle, and the crowd of newspaper men and women and the Governor's car, with the uniformed chauffeur up in front, were no longer visible. Miss Pickerell, looking through the dusty windows, could see only the clouds as the plane rose swiftly above them.

"Yes," she sighed, patting Nancy Agatha softly on her head, "yes, we're off."

4
"A Most Disagreeable Journey"

Nancy Agatha wasn't the least bit interested in the cargo plane. She glanced around to make sure that Miss Pickerell sat nearby and promptly went to sleep.

Miss Pickerell couldn't say that the plane impressed her very much either. There was absolutely nothing to look at, except the pilot's closed door up in front, and that didn't really count. There weren't even any interesting packages, some that perhaps couldn't be fitted into the hold, stowed on the floor. She, Euphus, and the Governor, tightly strapped into their hard metal seats, with the cow in the trailer directly behind them, were the only passengers.

"I suppose that's because it's a specially chartered plane," Miss Pickerell said to herself. "People in the television industry can afford to pay for this sort of thing."

She remembered a story in one of the free

magazines she had picked up in the supermarket. She had taken the trouble to read it since it was all about Rosemary's favorite television actor. The amount of money he earned was repeated four times in the story.

"I couldn't even sell my entire farm for what he earns in one night," she murmured.

"What did you say?" the Governor, sitting on her right-hand side, asked quickly.

"Nothing," Miss Pickerell told him. "I think we can take our seat belts off now."

"The 'Fasten Your Seat Belts' sign went off fifteen minutes ago," Euphus, sitting on the other side, told her.

Miss Pickerell consulted her watch. It was nearly five o'clock.

"Is it five-and-a-half or six-and-a-half hours to London, Euphus?" she asked. "Do you know exactly?"

"Of course I know," Euphus replied. "But it will be longer with this plane. It's just crawling."

"Perhaps cargo planes fly slower," the Governor suggested. "They may not have the latest equipment."

"This one looks ancient," Euphus complained. "It'll take eight hours, I bet."

"Then we'll be in London before one in the

morning," Miss Pickerell said, calculating quickly.

"Before one in the morning, Square Toe County time," Euphus corrected her. "Before seven in the morning, London time. There's a six-hour difference. That's because the earth turns and we're—"

"I'm a little hungry," the Governor interrupted, sighing. "Don't they serve dinner on this plane?"

"Nope," Euphus said. "There's no kitchen. There's no movie, either."

Miss Pickerell adjusted her watch to make it show English time. Then she reached up for the knitting bag she had placed on the shelf above her.

"I have some sandwiches," she said. "Mrs. Pickett brought them. She told me there were chicken and egg salad and tuna fish."

The Governor ate one of each. Euphus bit into an egg salad sandwich and said he wished it were peanut butter. Miss Pickerell, who did not feel very hungry, had half of a tuna fish sandwich. The Governor took the other half.

"I feel much better now," he said, when he finished. "I'll start preparing my speech. I have a few ideas about inflation that I want to share with the British public."

"Me, I'm going to look out of the other windows," Euphus announced.

Miss Pickerell didn't believe he would see any more than the darkening sky out of any of the windows. But she did not comment.

"I wish I could think of something to do, myself," she sighed, as she stood up to brush the crumbs off her blue serge skirt and sat down again. "I certainly don't want to read the minutes that Mr. Sweeney wrote in the diary. And there's nothing special I want to put in about the trip yet. Maybe I ought to knit for a while."

She gave up that idea when she looked at the half-finished scarf she was making for Rosemary. Miss Tackintosh, of the WHY NOT KNIT IT DEPARTMENT in the Square Toe City General Store, had sold her the wool and given her the pattern.

"It's very fashionable," she had said to Miss Pickerell.

Rosemary didn't think so at all.

"That stitch went out of style two years ago," she told Miss Pickerell, when she showed her the first five rows. "And nobody wears that color any more."

Miss Pickerell had kept on knitting because she thought the style might change. But it hadn't so far. She felt very discouraged.

She put the scarf away and searched in her

knitting bag for the peppermint drops she had remembered to take at the very last minute. She had stuffed them into the bag, together with Mrs. Broadribb's second-best bird-watching glasses and the present that Mr. Rugby had given her. Euphus came running when he saw her take out the peppermint drops. He also insisted on opening Mr. Rugby's package.

"Want to play a game?" he asked, as he showed her the two packs of playing cards inside. "Want to play double solitaire? We can spread the cards out on the floor."

Miss Pickerell examined her watch. Only three hours and fourteen minutes had passed since they boarded.

"All right," she sighed. "One game."

They played four games. Euphus and Miss Pickerell won two each. Euphus wanted to play another. Miss Pickerell didn't feel like stooping over the floor any more.

"I'm tired," she said. "I'm going to stretch out and relax."

She leaned back in her seat and thought about England.

"I could have looked everything up in the encyclopedia before I left," she said to herself. "Oh, well, I'll just have to review in my mind what I *do* know."

She thought about Queen Victoria first, the

queen who lived in the nineteenth century and wore those little bonnets with the veils hanging down in the back. Mr. Trilling, Square Toe City's piano tuner, had fixed up his front parlor to resemble what he called the Victorian Age. Personally, Miss Pickerell thought that the plush curtains and the lace doilies and all the little ornaments he had everywhere made the room seem smaller. But Mr. Trilling said that was the Victorian look.

She racked her brains to remember something else about Queen Victoria, but all she could recall was that her husband's name was Albert. She decided to think about King Henry VIII instead. He lived long before Queen Victoria and had six wives, some of whom he had beheaded, and he had a daughter, called Elizabeth, who had red hair and who later became Queen Elizabeth I and . . .

The pictures in Miss Pickerell's mind were becoming more and more blurred. She had to concentrate hard so that she wouldn't mix Elizabeth up with Mary, her half-sister, who did not want her to be queen. And she had a very difficult time figuring out the arguments between them.

She was just trying to unravel a most dangerous plot against Elizabeth and getting extremely worried about what would happen next when she felt someone violently shaking her shoulders.

"Better wake up, Miss Pickerell!" the Gover-

nor was shouting. "This plane is CRASHING!! It won't be long now. It—"

The plane was indeed behaving in a very strange way, Miss Pickerell realized the instant she got her senses together. It seemed actually to be jumping around in mid-air. And it was shaking so hard, she could feel the vibrations going up through the soles of her feet. Even on her trips to Mars and the Moon, nothing like this had ever happened.

"Forevermore!" she breathed. "Euphus! Where's Euphus?"

Euphus was sitting right beside her, bouncing happily up and down in his seat.

"Fasten your seat belt," she told him sternly, while she took an anxious look at her cow.

"What's the use of fastening a seat belt when a plane is crashing?" the Governor asked.

But he tried nervously to tighten his own seat belt. His fingers trembled and, as he bent forward, his top hat began sliding down one side of his head and his shoulders got hunched up nearly to his ears.

"Pooh!" Miss Pickerell told him, hoping she sounded a great deal more confident than she personally felt. "It's—it's probably only a storm."

"It's turbulence," Euphus, still bouncing, announced. "That's the motion caused by the vertical currents resulting from surface cooling of the air that—"

"If it *is* turbulence," the Governor interrupted in his most dignified voice, "all I can say is that we have a very poor pilot. I can understand now why he hasn't shown his face even once during the trip. Look out of your window, Euphus. He is about to bump us into some trees."

"We're landing!" Euphus shouted.

"Certainly not a smooth landing," the Governor added.

Miss Pickerell examined her watch again. It was 5:15 A.M. No wonder there was light outside the windows now. She leaned as far forward as she could over Euphus's head to look out.

"My!" she whispered, peering down at the small houses they were flying over, every single one with a chimney somewhere on its roof. "London's a city of chimney tops."

"Not on my side," the Governor stated. "I see skyscrapers."

The plane was getting ready to land. Miss Pickerell could tell by the changing sound of the engines. The hard bump on the ground came the very next minute and the plane began moving along the runway and on to the disembarkation point. It traveled at dizzying speed.

Miss Pickerell closed her eyes. She also put her hands over the buzzing sound in her ears.

"I know how you feel," the Governor said sympathetically. "It has been a disagreeable journey, altogether a most disagreeable journey!"

5
Something Is Wrong

Miss Pickerell unfastened her seat belt the instant the wheels stopped turning. She rushed over to Nancy Agatha immediately.

"We've arrived," she told her, while she inspected her carefully to make absolutely sure that she was none the worse for her journey. "And in just a few seconds you'll be outside in the good fresh air."

Euphus and the Governor joined Miss Pickerell in the automobile. She backed the car and the trailer out of the plane when a young man in white overalls placed a ramp at the rear door. A young woman in blue overalls steered her politely in the direction of the airport.

"The picture postcards I've seen of the Heathrow Airport must have been made up," she remarked to Euphus and the Governor as she kept driving and looking around. "They showed shops and magazine stands and even a moving sidewalk. I remember that one especially because it—"

"This is the cargo airport," Euphus interrupted. "You don't think they'd let a cow go through the regular place, do you?"

"My cow can go anywhere," Miss Pickerell retorted indignantly.

"Personally, I find it highly disrespectful," the Governor commented. "I believe I will say something to that effect to the proper authorities. Or perhaps I will mention it in—"

"Paging Miss Pickerell!" a voice called out on a loudspeaker. "Paging Miss Pickerell, her cow, Euphus, and the Governor! Mr. Cyril Chuff-Cooper is waiting for you directly in back of Customs and Immigration, next to Gate Seven."

Mr. Cyril Chuff-Cooper was a tall man with thinning red hair, who wore a short tan raincoat and had a dark green muffler wrapped around his neck. Miss Pickerell noticed, when she got closer, that he had a very worried expression on his face. The expression changed to a smile when he saw her. And he ran forward to shake hands the minute the Customs and Immigration inspectors had taken a long silent look at Miss Pickerell and her cow, scrutinized the passports and the special permit from the Ministry of Agriculture, Fisheries, and Food, and allowed the automobile and the trailer to pass through.

"Ah, Miss Pickerell!" Mr. Chuff-Cooper exclaimed. "And Euphus! And the Governor! And the cow, of course! Mr. Piffle telephoned to tell me about all of you. I trust you had a pleasant journey."

The Governor opened his mouth to tell him something about the trip, but Mr. Cyril Chuff-Cooper did not give him a chance to start.

"I have booked you into a hotel that I'm sure you will enjoy," he went on, talking even faster than Mr. Piffle. "And I have arranged for the cow—Nancy Agatha, isn't it?—to be sheltered in the kitchen garden next door. It's a very large garden with a green apple tree and plenty of grass. It is also bounded by a high wall and it has a shed for bad weather. She will be perfectly safe and happy there. And now, we'll push off, shall we?"

He walked ahead to a small car parked outside. He turned to add some directions before he climbed in.

"Just follow me," he called. "It's a longish ride, but I'll get you there in no time. And don't forget to drive the *English* way, on the *left* side of the road!"

Miss Pickerell did not even have a chance to tell him about driving slowly. And when they

started, she could not take her eyes off the road for a second. She had to concentrate on staying on what she kept thinking was the *wrong* side. Everything got still more complicated when Mr. Cyril Chuff-Cooper led her off the main highway and onto the twists and turns of the streets of London. Once she nearly lost him as

they got separated by a red double-decker bus. But Euphus spotted him and Miss Pickerell drove on, while the Governor commented on the rows of neat houses and gardens they were passing and talked about the people who stopped to stare at Nancy Agatha and the trailer. Miss Pickerell would have liked, at least, to catch a glimpse of the gardens. But she gritted her teeth and drove on.

She was almost ready to collapse with relief when Mr. Cyril Chuff-Cooper slowed down and she followed him up a circular driveway to the revolving glass doors of a hotel entrance. She was also ready to give him a good piece of her mind. But he spoke first.

"My mate here," he said, leaning out of his car and smiling at the red-faced doorman at the same time that he handed him a fistful of coins, "my mate here will get you nice and settled. I expect you all want some breakfast."

"They do a very good steak-and-kidney pie here," the doorman suggested, while he politely opened the door for Miss Pickerell and helped her out of the automobile.

"This is the start of our cricket season," Mr. Chuff-Cooper went on. "The hotel can get you some tickets."

"I don't know about the gentlemen," the doorman said. "The lady might prefer the cinema."

"And there are the tours for visitors," Mr. Chuff-Cooper continued. "They can take you to see the changing of the Guard at Buckingham Palace or to Trafalgar Square to see the statue of Lord Nelson or to . . ."

Miss Pickerell stared, open-mouthed. She

and her cow had traveled 3,000 miles on a dirty, uncomfortable cargo plane to lead a parade for the International Antique Car Fair. And here was Mr. Cyril Chuff-Cooper, the managing agent of that parade, not saying a word about it. Why, he was actually dreaming up things for her to do, instead. What's more, he wasn't even asking the Governor for the last-minute instructions from Mr. Piffle, those instructions that Mr. Piffle had considered so urgent.

"See here!" she said. "I—"

Mr. Cyril Chuff-Cooper did not let her interrupt. He went on talking about the sights of London, while he gradually slid away from the window and eased himself back behind the wheel.

"Wait!" Miss Pickerell cried out, when she saw him starting to put the car into gear. "You haven't told me about the parade."

"Tomorrow," Mr. Chuff-Cooper called back from the car that was already speeding down the driveway. "I'll phone you tomorrow."

Miss Pickerell stood watching the disappearing Mr. Cyril Chuff-Cooper. Something was *wrong,* she knew. She felt it in her bones. But what? Euphus and the Governor, still sitting in the automobile, didn't seem concerned. They were asking the doorman to be sure to put them into the best rooms. The doorman nodded, as he called for a porter to carry up Euphus's duffel bag and the Governor's shining leather case.

"And now you, Miss," he said. "We'll be getting you upstairs, too."

"I'd rather take my cow into the garden first," Miss Pickerell told him.

She walked slowly with Nancy Agatha to the kitchen garden where a porter led her. She sat down under the green apple tree to think. The cow lay down beside her.

"Nothing ever turns out exactly the way you expect it to," Miss Pickerell observed, while she stroked her cow's neck and listened to her contented mooing. "Or does it? Anyway, almost nothing . . ."

6
Miss Pickerell Hears the News

Miss Pickerell's room in the hotel was exactly the kind that she liked. It had pale pink wallpaper with rows of forget-me-nots running up and down, a thick matching carpet, and a large framed picture of a kitten, playing with a ball of yarn, hanging over the bed. Everything looked as neat as a pin. And there was a wide window, overlooking a green, leafy park.

The boy in the brass-buttoned uniform who carried up her umbrella, her knitting bag, and her valise checked twice to be sure there were fresh towels in the bathroom and plenty of hangers in the closet. He drew Miss Pickerell's attention to the list of important hotel telephone numbers under the glass top that covered the brown wooden bureau. Before he left, he pointed with pride to the television set that stood opposite the bed.

"We get American television shows in London now," he said. "On our third channel."

He turned the set on to demonstrate the fact. Miss Pickerell turned it off the minute he was outside the door. She walked over to the window to take a good look at the park. It was only eight o'clock in the morning, but mothers and children were already enjoying themselves there. One small girl with bright red ribbons in her hair was having a very exciting time romping after her dog. Miss Pickerell frowned when she saw another child about to step into a carefully arranged flower bed. But the child moved away quickly when her mother called out and gave her a firm look. Miss Pickerell nodded approvingly.

"That's the way to bring up children," she said to herself. "They need to learn respect for beautiful things. Now I'd better start unpacking."

She had just finished hanging up the two dresses that Rosemary had placed in her valise and was in the middle of putting away Mrs. Broadribb's second-best bird-watching glasses when she realized how hungry she was. Her stomach felt absolutely empty.

"But I won't go down to the dining room," she decided. "I'll telephone Room Service for some breakfast. And I'll have it right here in front of the window."

The Room Service number was the first one on her bureau-top list. She called immediately and asked for orange juice, scrambled eggs, and coffee.

"You're also entitled to toast on that breakfast, Madam," the polite voice at the other end of the wire informed her. "Or hot jam pastries. Those are really very nice."

Miss Pickerell thought she would take a chance on the recommendation.

"The hot jam pastries," she said. "As quickly as possible, please,"

She sat down to figure out the time it must be on her farm while she waited. If she subtracted six hours from the 8:24 that her watch now showed, it would be only after two in the morning on Square Toe Mountain. That was too early to call Mr. Kettelson.

"I think I'd better call Euphus and the Governor and see how they're getting along," she reflected. "I have their room numbers in my knitting bag."

She was unfolding the piece of paper that had the room numbers on it when her breakfast arrived. It came on a wheeled cart laden with silver-covered dishes to keep everything hot and a napkin made of real linen. Miss Pickerell ate slowly, enjoying every mouthful. She especially liked the hot jam pastries. She made a mental note to be sure to get the recipe before she left.

"And now," she said, when she finished, "I think I'll go for a walk in that lovely park, that is, as soon as I call Euphus and the Governor again." But neither of them answered the telephone.

Miss Pickerell straightened her hat, which she had forgotten to take off, took her sweater and umbrella along because everybody said that it was always cold and rainy in London, and went down in the self-service elevator. Except for the reception clerk standing behind his high desk and a middle-aged lady in a tweed jacket sitting on a leather couch, the lobby was deserted. Miss Pickerell marched through the revolving doors, said, "No, thank you," to the doorman who asked if she required a taxi, and crossed the street into the park.

"Forevermore!" she whispered, as she inhaled great breaths of soft fresh air and gazed at the flower beds that stretched out as far as she could see ahead of her. "It's even better than I expected."

There were irises and peonies and foxgloves and huge boughs of rhododendrons and enormous trees that cast dappled shadows on the grass around them. Miss Pickerell walked on and on, feeling more wonderful every minute.

"It's so peaceful!" she kept saying to herself. "So peaceful and so quiet and so far away from . . . from *everything!*"

But London burst upon her with a roar when she came to the far end of the park. She was now facing a city street, with crowded sidewalks, people rushing in and out of shops, and cars, trucks, and buses lumbering their way through the heavy traffic. A farmer in a wagon piled high with cabbages and apples was stuck in the middle of the street. He kept urging his horse to cross to the other side. The horse, much too frightened to move, stood shivering, rooted to the spot.

"No! No!" Miss Pickerell screamed to the very tall policeman, his stick lifted over his head, who seemed to appear from nowhere and came racing in the direction of the horse. "Don't hit him! Please! Please!"

The policeman was only raising his stick to stop the traffic, however. When every car, bus, and truck had come to a screeching halt, he walked over to the horse and gently led him across the street. Miss Pickerell applauded loudly. The policeman smiled and tipped back his helmet. Miss Pickerell could see that he had brown curly hair. She also thought that he had a very boyish smile.

"It was kind of you to help that frightened animal," she told him, when he joined her on the sidewalk. "Very kind indeed."

"Somebody had to," the policeman replied, blushing a little.

"Yes," Miss Pickerell agreed. "But I believe you noticed, Officer . . ."

She paused to hear his name.

"Simpson," the officer told her. "Reginald Simpson. I'm a London constable. I—"

He interrupted himself to peer into her face.

"You're Miss Pickerell!" he exclaimed. "I thought I recognized you. Your picture has been in all our papers. And the picture of your cow, too. She has a beautiful coat."

"She is also a very alert and intelligent animal," Miss Pickerell told him. "I'm going back now to talk to her for a while. She doesn't like to be alone too long."

Officer Simpson turned with Miss Pickerell when she started walking back to the hotel. Marching up and down the park was part of his daily job routine, he explained.

"It's too bad about that antique car fair," he remarked, after they had proceeded a few steps.

Miss Pickerell stopped short instantly.

"What's too bad about the antique car fair?" she asked.

"Why, the news about the earthquake," the constable replied. "It's been on television for hours."

Miss Pickerell didn't take the time to tell him

that she was not a regular television watcher.

"What earthquake?" she inquired.

Officer Simpson opened his eyes wide in amazement.

"The earthquake in our North Sea," he said. "As far as I know we've *never* had an earthquake there before. And the movement seems to have damaged our oil wells there. People say it will take months to put them right again."

Miss Pickerell felt herself beginning to lose patience.

"I would like to get back to the subject of the antique car fair," she said.

"But that *is* the subject," the constable told her. "Until the oil wells are repaired, we are all going to be on very strict fuel rations, much too strict to permit the luxury of a motor parade. The antique car fair has been postponed, Miss Pickerell, indefinitely postponed."

"Postponed?" Miss Pickerell breathed. "*Indefinitely* postponed?"

"From what I hear on the telly," Officer Simpson went on apologetically, "our other oil sources are running low. They say that's true in your country too and that you also may have to . . ."

Miss Pickerell walked over to the nearest park bench. She sat down heavily. Two tame squirrels came to perch themselves on the bench with her. Miss Pickerell gave them only a passing glance. She was too busy pulling her thoughts together. She *knew* now why Mr. Cyril Chuff-Cooper had that worried expression on his face. She *knew* why he had hurried away, saying only that he would call her tomorrow. What could she do now to save the Home for Retired and Disabled Animals? What could she do now for the animals who had nobody to depend on for their future but herself, and she . . . she . . . ?

She leaned over to touch the squirrels and tried to choke back her sobs. If Officer Simpson, shuffling his feet in embarrassment, had not been standing right there, she would have cried out loud.

7
Chin Up!

Miss Pickerell sat in the garden near Nancy Agatha and thought very gloomy thoughts. She was careful not to let her cow realize this. Animals, she knew, were quick to sense the feelings of people around them. And she definitely did not want Nancy Agatha to become as depressed as she was.

"Oh, well," she sighed finally, "I suppose I ought to get back to the hotel and explain the situation to Euphus and the Governor. Of course, they may have already heard all about it on television. Certainly, Euphus—"

She leaped to her feet when she suddenly remembered that she had not seen hide or hair of Euphus since their arrival.

"And that boy," she murmured, as she sped toward the revolving glass doors, "can get into more mischief in one minute than any *ten* boys of his age. With his imagination, there's just no telling what he may be up to."

The doorman, when she asked him about Euphus, said that he was in the lounge, to the right of the lobby.

"Your nephew is having himself a squash, Miss," he told her. "Upon my recommendation. It's a lovely drink for young people, made with water and sweet orange syrup. Very delicious!"

Miss Pickerell found Euphus at the far end of the lounge. He was sitting at a low table that had a tray, two bottles, and a tall glass on it. His eyes were glued to the lounge television set.

"I know," he said, when Miss Pickerell joined him. "The Governor knows, too. And Mr. Cyril Chuff-Cooper hasn't called."

"He was not supposed to telephone until tomorrow," Miss Pickerell reminded him.

"He won't," Euphus replied, while he took another sip of his orange squash. "He's lost his job, I think. The headquarters office of the International Antique Car Fair is closed. The Governor found out about that. The Governor said that we would have to leave soon and he had a lot of things to attend to first. He went to see—"

Miss Pickerell wasn't the least bit interested at the moment in whom the Governor had gone to see. She had something completely different on her mind that she wanted to talk about.

"Euphus," she interrupted, "didn't you tell me that you had a solution for the energy crisis?"

"Not the *whole* energy crisis," Euphus replied. "I told you that the fuel substitute could be used in cars and that it's a new science idea and . . ."

"Tell me again," Miss Pickerell asked. "Tell me again, now."

"O.K.," Euphus sighed. "To begin with, there's gasoline and gasohol. Gasohol is a mixture of about ninety per cent gasoline and ten per cent alcohol. The alcohol part is called ethanol or ethyl alcohol."

"I see," Miss Pickerell said. "Now, can you tell me how this ethanol is made, how long it takes, and just how one uses such a substitute fuel oil? Can you do this quickly and briefly, Euphus?"

"Easy!" Euphus replied. "It's made just like wine by the fermentation of natural sugars and starches. The yeast cells that grow on the crushed grape skins produce an enzyme called zymase. Zymase acts on the sugar in the grapes and the result is fermentation into alcohol. Simple! Only I don't know how long it takes. I do know, though, that it doesn't have to be grapes. You can add yeast to all sorts of things. To garbage, too."

"Enzymes?" Miss Pickerell questioned. "The organic substances in living cells that can cause chemical change? The ones I read about in your biology book?"

Euphus nodded.

"And as I said," he went on, "it's simple. You just pour the gasohol or the ethanol into the tank the way you do gasoline. My biology teacher says that people are beginning to use gasohol but that gasohol isn't really as good as ethanol because it doesn't save as much gas."

"How much gas does gasohol save?" Miss Pickerell asked.

"I told you," Euphus answered. "Only ten per cent. My teacher says that's something, but almost nothing compared to ethanol, which is a hundred per cent alcohol. And he says that ethanol improves combustion efficiency and that it pollutes the air even *less* than unleaded gasoline, since only water and harmless carbon dioxide are produced when it's burned and that . . . oh, lots of other things.

"When do we leave England, Aunt Lavinia? The Governor promised to take me to see a pizza factory I found out about when he comes back."

"You can tell the Governor that we are not leaving England just yet," Miss Pickerell said firmly, as she began walking out of the lounge and toward the revolving glass doors.

"Where are you going?" Euphus called after her.

"Where every American who has a problem goes for assistance," Miss Pickerell called back and, in almost the same breath, added to the driver in the taxi outside, "to the American Embassy."

"You can really walk there," the driver told her. "It's a very short distance."

"I'd rather ride," Miss Pickerell said. "It will be faster."

She told the driver to keep the change from the four half-crowns she gave him when he pulled up in front of the American Embassy. She took the time to observe that the Embassy was a large, very important-looking building and that it also faced a park. Once inside, she had only the impression of corridors and turnings and doors that blurred into confusion, as she kept asking for the American Ambassador and receiving startled looks and wrong directions in return.

"This is ridiculous!" she exclaimed out loud, when she landed behind a staircase and practically fell into the arms of a cleaning woman who was working there with a vacuum and a floor-polishing mop. The cleaning woman didn't seem very surprised.

"Lost, are you?" she asked. "I'd try the office directly above, if I was you, love, the one that has the posters of American rivers on all the walls. The girl with the yellow corkscrew curls in there knows everything. And she'll treat you like a lady."

The girl with the corkscrew curls, Miss Pickerell noticed when she found her, now had dark auburn hair. She was very sympathetic when

Miss Pickerell explained why she *had* to see the American Ambassador.

"I understand," she said to Miss Pickerell. "But the person you want to see is not the American Ambassador. It's one of the Advisors on British Affairs to the American Ambassador that you need. Come, Miss Pickerell, you've done enough running around. I'll take you to Sir Wilfred, the Right Honorable Sir Wilfred White. He'll be able to advise you."

The Right Honorable Sir Wilfred White was an elderly gentleman with a military moustache that was turning gray and huge horn-rimmed glasses that rested on a long, beaklike nose. He rose from the swivel chair behind his desk when the girl with the curls introduced Miss Pickerell.

"Ah, yes, of course, Miss Pickerell," he said. "I've seen your picture in the papers. May I offer you some tea? No? Well, then do sit down and tell me what has brought you here."

He listened quietly while she told him about the Home for Retired and Disabled Animals and about what Assistant Sheriff Swiftlee had said at the meeting in the library and then about Mr. Anthony Piffle and Mr. Cyril Chuff-Cooper and finally about Euphus and the ethanol and gasohol.

"With ethanol," she said, drawing in a deep

breath and summing everything up, "or even with gasohol, the automobile, at least, can keep running. And the International Antique Car Fair won't have to be canceled. And I will be able to save the animals. It's all very simple."

Sir Wilfred looked at her thoughtfully.

"I've heard about these recommendations for fuel substitutes," he said. "I don't rightly know why they haven't been given more consideration. But . . ."

He paused, while he pushed his swivel chair back and crossed and uncrossed his long legs.

"But," he went on, "even should I wish to help you get this . . . this scheme of yours started, Miss Pickerell, which, I assure you, I most fervently do, I cannot. It is not my department."

"Not your department?" Miss Pickerell gasped.

"No," Sir Wilfred said.

He got up and walked toward the window. He pulled the heavy curtains aside and looked out.

"On a beautiful spring day," he said slowly, "one wishes it were possible to see the Thames from here. It would be a lovely sight. Have you seen our Thames River yet, Miss Pickerell?"

Miss Pickerell could only shake her head. The Right Honorable Sir Wilfred White had the strangest way of flitting from one subject to another. He . . .

"Our Houses of Parliament stand just beside the Thames," he went on. "We have two of them, the House of Lords and the House of Commons."

"We have two in Washington, too," Miss Pickerell told him. "The Senate and the House of Representatives."

"I know," Sir Wilfred smiled. "In any case, questions of the type you have raised, questions about plans relating to the energy crisis, are decided in those two Gothic buildings at the foot of the Thames. The debates down there, particularly in our House of Commons, determine our national policy. I would go so far as to say that they often dictate the destiny of our nation for centuries to come."

"Yes," Miss Pickerell said respectfully.

Sir Wilfred turned from the window and walked back to his desk.

"I can do only one thing for you, Miss Pickerell," he said. "I can write to my representative in Parliament and ask him to take the matter up in Committee. If the Committee agrees, the subject will then come before the House for debate."

Miss Pickerell looked up with sudden eagerness.

"That sort of process takes months, however, I'm afraid," Sir Wilfred continued. "House debates are fixed long beforehand and . . ."

He stopped to glance at Miss Pickerell, who had slumped dejectedly down in her chair.

"Are you sure you won't change your mind about the tea?" he asked gently. "We Britishers believe that it . . . it helps."

Miss Pickerell smiled faintly.

"No, thank you," she said, gathering up her knitting bag and her umbrella. "And thank you for your kind interest."

"It's you who are kind, Miss Pickerell," Sir Wilfred said, walking to the door and holding it open for her. "I can understand your concern. I keep dogs myself."

He stood watching, as she moved slowly down the corridor.

"Look after yourself, Miss Pickerell," he called. "And don't forget! Keep the chin up!!"

8
Miss Pickerell Gives Parliament a Piece of Her Mind

The taxi driver who was taking her back to the hotel already had his hands on the wheel when Miss Pickerell changed her mind.

"To the House of Commons!" she shouted, so that he would be sure to hear her across the brightly polished glass panel that separated the front from the back of the taxi. "The House of Commons on the Thames."

The driver turned around curiously. He slid the panel to one side.

"Pardon me for asking, Miss," he said, "but do you have an appointment there?"

"No," Miss Pickerell admitted. "I can get in, though, can't I?"

"Not on the Floor of the House," he told her, as he started to drive. "Not where they do the debating. Nobody's allowed there, not even the wives or husbands or sweethearts. They sit in the Strangers' Gallery."

"Oh!" Miss Pickerell exclaimed.

"I sat in the Strangers' Gallery myself once," the driver commented. "I had to be quiet as a mouse. Afraid to open my mouth, I was. Afraid that the whips would get me, if I said a word."

"The whips!" Miss Pickerell whispered.

"Oh, not real whips," the driver explained. "Not the kind that put lashes on your back. These are just as bad, though, to my way of thinking. They're the gents who keep the House members in line, make sure they vote the way their Party wants them to. And there's the Sergeant-at-Arms. They do say that he can lock people up in the Victoria Tower when they don't behave. But I don't rightly know if that's true. Here you are, Miss. Here's Parliament Square and the door to the Strangers' Gallery. And you can see our clock tower, the one with the clock we call Big Ben on it."

Miss Pickerell looked out at the massive gray buildings and up at all the spires and towers on top of them. A flag flew high above one of the towers, she saw.

"That's our Union Jack," the driver said proudly. "When the flag's up there, it means the House is sitting. You're in luck, Miss, if that's what you've come here for. You'll be able to hear the debating."

The attendant who let Miss Pickerell in directed her to a waiting room. A man with a great gold medal dangling over his stomach asked her if she had a ticket. Then he stared at her hat, her knitting bag, and her umbrella, murmured, "Ah, Miss Pickerell," and signaled for her to follow him. He escorted her to the highest gallery she had ever seen and seated her between a man with a stiff derby hat on his lap and a young woman who kept her eyes fixed on the right side of the Floor.

"I guess she's one of the sweethearts that the taxi driver mentioned," Miss Pickerell said to herself.

She leaned as far forward as she could to get a good view. The Floor of the House, she saw, was divided into two parts, with a carpet running down the middle. There were benches on both sides of the carpet. The members of the House sat on the benches. Some had hats on and some put their hats on their heads the minute they got up to say something. They always began by asking permission from a man who wore a black-and-gold robe over his suit and had a grayish wig hanging down to his shoulders. They addressed him as Mr. Speaker and he seemed very important. Miss Pickerell thought for a moment of seeking him out in his dressing room or wherever he would go later to take off his wig and discussing her problem with him. She dismissed the idea as impractical.

"That Sergeant-at-Arms would never let me," she sighed. "I . . . I really don't know why I asked the taxi driver to bring me here, except that maybe I didn't know what else to do. I'll listen for a little while longer and then I'll leave."

She gave her attention to the member who had just gotten up to speak.

"It is the view of my Party," he said, "that solar energy is the only solution. We must proceed with the utmost concentration to develop this resource. The unfortunate accident in our North Sea area only highlights the importance of this development. My Party, in making this recommendation, has naturally the best interests of the country at heart."

A member from the benches on the other side rose to his feet.

"The welfare of the nation is the deep concern of the Opposition Party as well," he said. "We, too, support the budget for the development of solar energy and wish to go on record to that effect."

A member from the original side stood up.

HEAR HEAR !!
SHOCKING!
I SAY!
IS NOTHING SACRED?!

"This is indeed an inspiring moment," he said. "The common concern for our country has united us in—"

"Common concern for the country, indeed!" Miss Pickerell screamed, jumping up out of her seat. "You're not even taking the trouble to investigate the facts."

The girl sitting next to Miss Pickerell looked horrified. The man with the derby hat motioned for her to sit down. Miss Pickerell shivered. She had never intended to burst out in this way. She had never even *dared* to *think* of talking back to the British Parliament from the gallery of the House of Commons. But now that she had started, she couldn't stop. The indignation poured out of her.

"If you'd investigate them, the facts, I mean," she went on, "you'd know that you have to wait at least fifty years before you'll have nearly enough solar energy. What about developing new energy supplies for now? My middle nephew, Euphus, often says that this is the age of technology and discovery and that . . ."

"Hear! Hear!"

The voices rose from the Floor and echoed through the high-ceilinged gallery. Miss Pickerell paused for only an instant.

"Euphus believes," she continued, "that we should put ethanol into the automobiles instead of gasoline. I fully agree with him. And if you're as concerned as you say about the welfare of the country, I think you should too. Nobody wants fuel rationing. Nobody likes—"

"Hear! Hear!"

The voices echoed and re-echoed. The man

who had cautioned her to sit down clapped his hands and tossed his derby hat in the air.

"It's easy to make ethanol," Miss Pickerell shouted over the din. "You make it like wine, only you use surplus and waste products from the farms instead of grapes. You can use grapes, too, I suppose, if they happen to be surplus. And I can suggest left-over wheat and barley and cornstalks and even city garbage. Now, I don't doubt for a minute that a direct use of solar energy will be better in the long run. But this is *now*. And my friend Professor Humwhistel has definitely advised me that we don't have the knowledge to use enough of the solar energy now and probably won't have for about fifty years. But we certainly have enough waste around and we should, we most certainly should—"

She choked off the conclusion of her sentence when the man with the gold medal laid his hand on her arm.

"Are you taking me to the Tower?" she asked, looking up at him. "I don't care. I'll go. I'll—"

"Calm yourself, Madam," the man urged. "The Speaker is sending you up a note."

Miss Pickerell saw that the man with the long gray wig was sitting in his chair and that he had a piece of paper in his hand. The members from the front benches were standing behind the chair, talking to him. Every once in a while, he listened attentively to something one of them said and wrote it on the piece of paper. When he finished, he gave the note to an attendant who was waiting and waved for the members to return to their benches.

"He's probably having me arrested," Miss Pickerell murmured to herself. "Or he's asking me to leave the country. I can't even say I blame him. I would send away visitors who broke all the rules, too."

She held onto the handle of her umbrella with both hands to keep them from shaking so hard. She let go only when the attendant brought up the note and she had to open the envelope.

> Dear Madam, (she read)
>
> We quite understand how persons can become unusually disturbed about the issue of fuel rationing and we value your suggestions about the use of ethanol in car engines. All of this wants a bit of thinking about, however. The first step is to find a way of making *enough* ethanol quickly and economically. We hope that you can supply us with such a method and that we will be able to test it and proceed as quickly as possible to offer our motorists the substitute fuel that they need.

I remain, with good wishes for the success of an effort in which we are both vitally interested,

Yours most respectfully,

The signature was scrawled. Miss Pickerell could not read it. She could not feel very relieved, either. She had no idea as to how one went about developing a method for fast and economic mass production of ethanol. And if she did not find out soon, there would be no antique car parade and no more Home for Retired and Disabled Animals in Square Toe County.

"What do I do now?" she asked herself again and again, and went on to tell herself each time that she hadn't the slightest idea.

9

"Perhaps Madam Should Try a Balloon"

Miss Pickerell asked everybody she could think of where she might find out about the method that Parliament wanted. She asked the man with the gold medal who was escorting her out and the man with the derby hat who was leaving with her and the attendant who stood at the door and the taxi driver who took her back to the hotel. Nobody could tell her.

The hotel lobby was crowded when she entered. New guests, young and noisy and all carrying knapsacks across their shoulders, were jostling and pushing each other in front of the receptionist's desk. It was a new reception clerk, Miss Pickerell observed. He had a sour expression on his face and he wore a badge pinned to the lapel of his neat gray suit. The badge had his name, Mr. T. T. Tottingham, printed on it. Miss Pickerell waited until he had finished handing out the keys and room numbers to the new arrivals and asked him, too, about the method for making ethanol quickly, cheaply, and in large quantitites.

"I'm sure I don't know, Madam," he replied. "Will there be anything else?"

"No, thank you," Miss Pickerell said weakly.

Up in her room, she stood in front of the window and gazed wearily out at the park. Two rows of smiling young girls on horseback were riding down the bridle path. The horses, tossing their manes in the wind, seemed as gay and carefree as their riders.

"Oh, my poor Homer," Miss Pickerell cried. "What can I do to save you and the others at the Home for Retired and Disabled Animals? I feel helpless, helpless. . . ."

She wished Mr. Rugby, her old friend from the Square Toe County Diner, were with her. He was such a jolly man and he always managed somehow to cheer her up. Or Professor Humwhistel, who was such a good listener and who knew the answer to so many problems.

"Well, I can still talk to *him,*" Miss Pickerell decided suddenly, as a new idea struck her. "I can even ask him about the ethanol method. It is very possible that he has the information and can tell me. Or he can send it airmail, special delivery. That wouldn't take too long. I'll dial direct right now."

She followed the directions for overseas calling that were pasted onto the telephone and carefully dialed the international code, the country code, the city code, and Mr. Humwhistel's local telephone number. Nobody answered. She tried again, just in case she had made a mistake in dialing. There was no answer. She decided to call Mr. Kettelson.

"He can go out and look for Professor Humwhistel," she told herself, "that is, if it's all right to leave Pumpkins."

Mr. Kettelson answered on the first ring. He was delighted to hear from Miss Pickerell and told her immediately that Pumpkins was just fine.

"But I won't talk too long," he added. "International telephone calls are expensive."

He also said that he had grave doubts about whether Professor Humwhistel could be of any help, when Miss Pickerell explained about the ethanol problem.

"The Professor never mentions ethanol, Miss Pickerell," he advised her. "I don't personally believe he can give you much information."

"Please tell him, anyway," Miss Pickerell asked. "He can call me here, if he has anything to say. He can call *collect.*"

She gave Mr. Kettelson the telephone number and hung up. She was just deliberating about whether she ought to call Sir Wilfred or go and see him again when someone knocked on the door. It was Euphus and the Governor, returning from their trip to the pizza factory. The minute they finished telling her about it and she stopped moaning over the fact that Euphus had eaten nine sample pizza slices, she showed them the note from the Speaker.

"I was thinking of going over to the American Embassy to ask if anyone there might know," she said.

"I'm sure they don't," the Governor commented grimly. "I'd have heard about it. The Speaker would have heard about it, too."

"I've asked everybody," Miss Pickerell added. "I've even asked Mr. Kettelson to ask Professor Humwhistel to—"

"Why didn't you ask me?" Euphus interrupted. *"I know."*

Both Miss Pickerell and the Governor stared, first at him and then at one another. Euphus looked back calmly.

"I don't know any place right around here," he said. "But I know about the place in Nysse. That's the village in Normandy with the Farnier Fuel Farm in it. Mr. Farnier went to college with my biology teacher. Afterwards, Mr. Farnier went back home to manage the family farm and then he began to experiment with ethanol. Normandy has some of the best farmland in France, and he makes lots and lots of ethanol very, very fast, my teacher says, and he uses a special procedure that's cheap—and he's the *only* one who knows about it."

Miss Pickerell picked up the telephone again. "Please connect me with the Farnier Fuel Farm in Nysse, France," she said to the operator. "As fast as you can!"

But it was a recorded voice that answered after the connection was made. It spoke in French and then in another language that Miss Pickerell could not understand and then in English.

"Mr. Farnier will not discuss Formula X99 on the telephone," it said, over and over again. "Mr. Farnier will not discuss Formula X99 on the telephone. Mr. Farnier will not . . ."

"I could have told you that," Euphus, who was leaning over Miss Pickerell so that he could hear every word, announced. "Mr. Farnier doesn't want some people to know his secret method. And he thinks they may be listening."

"Who are the *some* people Mr. Farnier doesn't want to know about his method?" Miss Pickerell asked quickly.

Euphus didn't know. His teacher hadn't explained that part.

"This fear of wiretapping is really going too far," the Governor sighed. "Now, I believe that . . ."

Miss Pickerell paid no attention. She was thinking hard. France was right across the channel. Why, she could . . .

"I believe it's no more than a thirty-minute ride by plane," the Governor, who seemed to be reading her mind, remarked.

"There's also a ferryboat that goes across and when the sea is rough, everybody gets seasick," Euphus added. "And they were going to build a tunnel under the channel. They never got to it. Or, maybe they started and didn't go on. I don't remember. But . . ."

Miss Pickerell was no longer listening. She was racing out the door and across the corridor to the elevator. She marched directly up to the desk when she got downstairs.

Mr. T. T. Tottingham was alone again. He was leafing through the pages of a gardening catalogue and looking very bored. Miss Pickerell felt like telling him that he might find the information extremely interesting if he took the trouble to read it. But she did not want to waste any time.

"One round-trip plane ticket to France," she said. "Across your English Channel."

Mr. Tottingham gave her a brief glance.

"All British cross-channel planes have been grounded, Madam," he said.

"Grounded!" Miss Pickerell exclaimed. "That's impossible."

"We are in an energy crisis, Madam," Mr. Tottingham stated. "We have had to take steps to reduce the consumption of oil. Parliament has already voted to institute coupon rations and to limit the availability of petrol at filling stations."

"I know about filling stations," Miss Pickerell told him.

"Since our stockpiles are being exhausted," Mr. Tottingham went on, "our Parliament—"

"I know about Parliament, too," Miss Pickerell said.

"Our Parliament," Mr. Tottingham continued, ignoring her interruption, "has seen fit to ground the heavy, oil-consuming, cross-channel British planes."

"Very well, then," Miss Pickerell said quickly. "I will take a French plane. Or any plane I can board immediately."

Mr. T. T. Tottingham threw her a scornful look.

"Doesn't Madam read the newspapers?" he asked. "Our British cross-channel pilots are protesting this government action. They are picketing and not permitting passengers to board foreign planes. It seems a futile gesture, I must say, since they are not allowing the foreign planes to land in the first place."

Miss Pickerell gasped. But she did not allow herself to spend any time in thinking about this strike action.

"I will go on your cross-channel ferry then," she said. "It will take longer, I know, and there's the danger, I understand, of seasickness, but it will have to do."

"Ferry trips have also been canceled," Mr. Tottingham told her. "By our British Rail, which is considering the possibility of ocean pollution from the damaged oil wells. Will that be all, Madam?"

He did not wait for her to answer. He returned to his examination of the gardening catalogue.

Miss Pickerell did *not* intend to let Mr. Tottingham brush her aside so carelessly. She bent right over the gardening catalogue and stared straight up into his face.

"I am talking to you about an *emergency,* Mr. Tottingham," she said, her nose practically touching his. "And I am sure that there are ways of crossing the channel in an emergency. You would certainly find one for . . . for your Parliament, for example. I want the same cour-

tesy and consideration. I *expect* you to find *me* a way."

Mr. T. T. Tottingham slid himself and his catalogue as far back from Miss Pickerell's face as he could get. He lifted his eyes to the ceiling and smiled. He smiled so broadly that Miss Pickerell could see the gold fillings in some of his teeth.

"Perhaps," he said, without looking at her, "perhaps Madam should try a balloon."

He laughed out loud at his own joke. Miss Pickerell did not laugh with him.

10
Officer Simpson to the Rescue

Miss Pickerell didn't think that the idea was funny at all. At the moment, she knew of no better solution for her problem. The prospect of sitting in the basketlike contraption that hung down from a flying balloon, with maybe her legs dangling outside, made her extremely uneasy. But she took a deep breath, pushed back the glasses that had slipped way down on her nose when she leaned over the garden catalogue, and told herself not to think about the basket part for the time being.

"Mr. Tottingham!" she called to the reception clerk, who was now standing near the letter boxes with his back to her. "I'd like the names of some balloonists, please."

Mr. Tottingham slapped the mail he was looking at down on top of the boxes and walked over to her.

"Madam," he snapped, "I have never seen a

flying balloonist except in some old flicks at the cinema. And—"

"Evidently you don't read the newspapers very regularly, either," Miss Pickerell retorted instantly. "Otherwise, you would certainly have seen the pictures of the balloonist who flew across the Atlantic Ocean to—"

"And, as I was about to say," the receptionist went on, "I have no names of any balloonists in my files."

"Then I will look in your telephone directories," Miss Pickerell told him. "Please let me have the books that cover London and its outskirts."

She searched in all of them, one after another. She searched under B for *Balloonists* and, when she couldn't find anything there, under C for *Carriers,* and under A, for *Aircraft Carriers, Balloon Type.* She gave the telephone books back when she couldn't think of where else to look and walked slowly out of the lobby.

The doorman thought she wanted a taxi when she came through the front doors. He shook his head sadly.

"There's none to be seen around here, Miss," he sighed. "Most of them have run out of petrol, I expect. Taxis will be getting some special transport rations, but that won't be until tomorrow."

Miss Pickerell sighed with him.

"It's hard times we're having, Miss," he added. "We'll cope, though. We always have done."

Miss Pickerell nodded and crossed the street to the park. She wished she could feel half as hopeful about her own difficulties. All she felt at the moment was a mounting fury. Mr. Farnier's refusal to talk about his method over the telephone seemed to her plain ridiculous. He was entitled to his fears, though, she supposed. But she *knew* she could persuade him to tell her the secret once he saw her and she could explain her reasons to him very carefully. If only she could cross that silly little channel! If only she could find a way!!

She sat down on a bench to think. She leaned her head back against the wooden slats and watched two chirpy sparrows who were holding a very cheerful conversation at the top of a cherry tree.

"I'm glad someone is happy," she commented to herself.

The sparrows moved from the treetop and settled on a low branch that reached out toward the bordering footpath. They stayed only an instant, however. They flew off with a wild flutter of wings when a pair of heavy boots approached. Miss Pickerell looked up to see Officer Reginald Simpson marching toward her.

"Why, Miss Pickerell!" he said. "I am so pleased to see you again. I hope you have been having an agreeable time in London."

Miss Pickerell did not have the energy to tell him just how she had been spending her time.

"I am off duty now," the constable went on a little shyly. "I can show you around the city a bit, if you like."

He unstrapped his helmet and sat down.

"Most of our lady visitors like to buy dresses and things like that in London," he said. "I could take you to some of our fashionable shops. How would that suit you, Miss Pickerell?"

Miss Pickerell couldn't think of anything she wanted to do less. She didn't answer the constable's question.

"Do you know anything about flying balloons?" she asked, instead.

Officer Simpson seemed a little startled, but he replied almost immediately.

"A bit," he said. "I know that there are two kinds. There's the hot air balloon. That's the one where you burn a fuel and make the air inside the balloon lighter than the surrounding air. You do that when you want to inflate the balloon and get it to go up. When you want to come down, you spill the hot air out. And you and the balloon descend in a sort of parachute landing."

"A sort of parachute landing," Miss Pickerell

breathed, while she tried to forget about the feeling of butterflies in her stomach.

"The second kind," Officer Simpson continued, "is called, I think, a hydrogen balloon. It's the hydrogen that blows this type of balloon up and makes it rise. There's a gas valve somewhere that you operate with a rope. I imagine you let the hydrogen go out when you want to fly lower or to land."

"That sounds reasonable," Miss Pickerell observed.

"Some people say," the constable commented, "that the hydrogen balloon is more dangerous. They believe that hydrogen can be ignited by the electricity in thunder and cause a fire in the balloon. It may very well be true. Most balloons use helium instead of hydrogen today."

"A very sound idea," Miss Pickerell said.

Officer Simpson nodded emphatically.

"I knew a balloonist once," he recalled. "He used to fly over Hyde Park, advertising soap. Pears soap, I believe it was. There were pictures of the soap painted all over the balloon. He never had any accidents, Mr. Porridge didn't. He stayed right in the park where there was no danger of bumping into buildings. And he tied the balloon to a tree with a long, strong rope to make sure he didn't go any farther than he wanted. Mr. Porridge believes in being extra cautious. He uses helium, himself."

Miss Pickerell stopped leaning against the slats of the park bench.

"Then, when he finished that job," Officer Simpson told her, "he started taking people up for rides in the park. Half a crown, he used to charge, I remember. The kids loved it. The parents didn't, though. Some of them got together and put a stop to the whole thing. Too risky, they said it was. I don't know why they panicked. For three years Mr. Porridge took those children up for rides without any trouble."

A wild hope was springing up in Miss Pickerell's breast. If . . . if this Mr. Porridge . . .

"Officer Simpson," she asked instantly, "do you think your Mr. Porridge could take me across the English Channel in his balloon?"

The constable swallowed so hard that Miss Pickerell could see his Adam's apple move up and down in his throat.

"Never mind why," she told him. "I don't have time to go into details. I can assure you, however, that it is of the utmost importance."

"I—I'm not sure," he stammered. "His balloon is not a very big one. He used to deflate it, I recall, and pack it into the basket. If I remember correctly, he sometimes went home with it strapped to the roof of a car."

"I don't see that size has anything to do with the matter," Miss Pickerell replied. "Balloons float with the wind. And the wind velocity varies with the altitude."

The constable looked at her admiringly.

"I looked it up in the encyclopedia," Miss Pickerell explained, "when I read in the newspaper about the balloonist crossing the Atlantic. I also consulted the dictionary. Velocity means the speed and intensity of the wind."

"That's just it," Officer Simpson argued. "Channel winds can be rough. They can seriously damage a balloon."

"Not if you adjust the altitude at which you are flying," Miss Pickerell insisted. "The encyclopedia was very definite about that."

Officer Simpson still did not seem entirely convinced.

"I doubt that Mr. Porridge has flown a balloon since he gave up those half-crown rides," he said. "That was more than a year ago. Nearer to two, most likely. It may take him time to get the hang of it again."

"Not too long," Miss Pickerell answered, while she kept telling herself that this must be true. "Do you know where you can find Mr. Porridge, Officer Simpson?"

Officer Simpson grinned.

"There's a jolly good chance he's at his local

pub," he said. "The food's good and cheap and—"

"Please locate him for me," Miss Pickerell interrupted. "Tell him that I must, I absolutely must, leave today. As soon as possible."

"If . . . if you say so, Miss Pickerell," the constable replied.

"We fly from Heathrow, I suppose?" Miss Pickerell asked.

"Probably Gatwick for the channel crossing," Officer Simpson said. "I'll check it out for you. I'll let you know."

"And I'll take a taxi immediately," Miss Pickerell told him, as she quickly gathered her belongings and hastened to get up from the bench.

"You may not be able to do that today," the constable reminded her. "I'd best talk to the Metropolitan Police about borrowing a car. And some transport for Mr. Porridge and his balloon."

Miss Pickerell wondered if Officer Simpson would be very embarrassed if she kissed him. She had an idea that he might be and shook his hand instead.

"There is no time to be lost," she told him, "or I would explain it all to you. All I can say at this moment is that you are doing a very commendable thing."

"If you say so," the constable replied again.

Miss Pickerell began hurrying out of the park.

"I'm staying in that hotel," she called back, as she ran. "Right across the street. Please telephone me there."

"You can depend on it," Officer Simpson, running in the other direction, called after her. "Not to worry, Miss Pickerell. Not to worry at all!"

11
Enter Mr. Albert Angus Porridge

The telephone in Miss Pickerell's room began to ring the minute after she opened her door. She raced over to answer.

"Hello! Hello!" she said breathlessly.

"I am Mr. Henri Farnier," a pleasant-sounding man replied. "You are surprised to hear from me, Miss Pickerell, yes? It is because you have such a very persistent nephew. He will also cost you a fortune in telephone calls, I am afraid. He asked the telephone operator to connect him with every Farnier in the book until he reached me at my home, where the listing is in the name of Amelie, my wife. I must say that I found your nephew to be a most interesting conversationalist."

Miss Pickerell gave two quick gasps and decided to get to the point.

"About the ethanol?" she asked.

"I have already advised your nephew," Mr.

Farnier said, "that I will be very happy to have my research do some good in the world. I have been trying to keep it from the commercial enterprises, which will use it only for their own selfish interests. Their people have been hounding me, yes, hounding me, day and night. Your nephew wisely remarked, when I mentioned this to him, that the life of the idealistic pioneer is usually a difficult one."

"Oh?" Miss Pickerell exclaimed.

"But, no matter," Mr. Farnier went on. "I am prepared to let you have a copy of the manuscript describing the new procedure, which is too complicated to discuss over the telephone, in any case. I will also let you have a test tube containing a sample of my ethanol. It is a pity that you cannot come to see the large stainless-steel vats in which I am able to produce the vast quantities. But I understand that you are in a great hurry to give everything to the Speaker of the House of Commons so that he can proceed with tests immediately."

"Definitely!" Miss Pickerell replied. "I would also like to give him a much bigger amount of the ethanol. It seems to me more practical."

"As you like," Mr. Farnier laughed. "I wish I could make the delivery to you myself in London. Unhappily, I am too occupied with another experiment. There is also the problem of

plane landings, I understand. And crossings, too, I believe."

"I am coming by balloon," Miss Pickerell said promptly.

"Ah, yes," Mr. Farnier replied. "And with favorable winds, you will make good time. From Dover to the landing in Calais is a matter of only twenty-two miles. I will send my wife to Calais. She will be standing next to the Customs man. My wife has found my manuscript most interesting, as I hope you will, too, when you read it. But tell me, Miss Pickerell, how are you planning to return to London?"

"I beg your pardon?" Miss Pickerell asked.

"From Dover to Calais," Mr. Farnier explained, "the winds blow from behind, pushing the balloon, which is as it should be. From Calais to Dover is the opposite. A balloon cannot fly in the face of the wind, you realize."

Miss Pickerell did not answer. She was too stunned even to find her voice. She had not given a thought to the subject of wind direction. Officer Simpson hadn't mentioned it, either. Maybe he hadn't learned about winds in his geography class. Or maybe he had forgotten. But the balloonist would know. He would know that Dover was west of Calais and, if the winds blew from west to east, he would say that a return journey was impossible and he . . .

"Miss Pickerell!" Mr. Farnier said, sounding as though he was no longer sure that she was on the telephone. "Miss Pickerell!"

"Yes, Mr. Farnier," she replied, because she had to say something.

"Miss Pickerell," Mr. Farnier went on, "I have a new son-in-law with whom I am not on very good terms. We do not always agree about things."

"I see," Miss Pickerell said politely, though she couldn't at all see why Mr. Farnier was bringing his family affairs into the conversation.

"As a wedding present from his family," Mr. Farnier continued, "my son-in-law received a Hovercraft."

"A Hovercraft?" Miss Pickerell asked.

"Yes," Mr. Farnier said. "It is a vehicle that travels across water on a cushion of air which is provided by very large fans. It goes usually at the rate of forty miles an hour. It can get you back across the channel in about half an hour."

"Oh, please . . ." Miss Pickerell pleaded.

"I can assure you," Mr. Farnier added, "that my son-in-law will not take you back across the channel for my sake. But he may do so for the sake of the Home for Retired and Disabled Animals that your nephew told me about. Your nephew also told me about your cow, Nancy Agatha, and about your cat, Pumpkins."

Miss Pickerell wondered what else Euphus might have told Mr. Farnier, but she did not want to take the time to ask.

"My son-in-law spends most of his day talking to his own cat, Matilde," Mr. Farnier sighed. "It is a strange occupation for a grown man and it does not leave him many hours to earn a living."

Miss Pickerell was about to tell him that his son-in-law could easily work out a schedule that would give him a chance to earn a living as well as to talk to Matilde, but again she did not want to take the time. She told him instead that her good friend, Officer Reginald Simpson, would call to give him the exact time of her departure in the balloon. She also said that, if necessary, she would talk to the son-in-law *personally* about taking her back.

"I'm sure I can persuade him," she advised Mr. Farnier, "after I describe the helpless animals in the Home to him."

"Well then," Mr. Farnier replied, "let us hope that the waters will not be too rough for a Hovercraft. My wife will be able to direct you."

Miss Pickerell hung up the minute she thanked Mr. Farnier and ran as fast as she could to explain things to Nancy Agatha. The cow mooed gratefully when she saw Miss Pickerell enter the garden.

"I know you're lonely," Miss Pickerell told her, as she patted her head and adjusted the silver bell which had slipped over to the back. "And now I have to go away again. But I'll get Euphus to keep you company, I promise."

Both Euphus and the Governor were sitting on the edge of the leather sofa at the far end of the lobby. They jumped up the instant they saw Miss Pickerell.

"There's a telephone message for you, Miss

Pickerell," the Governor told her. "The clerk gave it to me in the hope that I would find you. Naturally, I haven't looked at it."

"Naturally," Miss Pickerell agreed, almost tearing the paper out of his hand and ignoring the shocked look on the Governor's face.

It was a message from the constable. The time he had called, 2:52 P.M., was neatly noted in the right-hand corner. He wanted her to know that he had made all arrangements and would be at the hotel with transport by approximately 3:15.

Miss Pickerell examined her watch. She did not answer the questioning look in the Governor's eyes.

"I must hurry," she told him. "Please excuse me, Governor. And Euphus, please go and talk to Nancy Agatha. Her pail is in the back of the shed, in case I don't get back in time to milk her."

She raced up the stairs to avoid waiting for the elevator. She took a moment to wrap a long scarf tightly around her hat and to drag her heaviest sweater out of the closet.

"It's better to be prepared," she told herself, as she ran down to the lobby again. "The constable said the winds could be bad."

Officer Simpson and another, even taller policeman were waiting at the foot of the stairs.

They walked on either side of her up to the revolving doors. Everybody in the lobby stared. They stared even harder when they saw the policemen escorting her into the automobile they had brought along.

"Forevermore!" Miss Pickerell gasped, when she took a look at the wire mesh that covered all the windows. "It's the wagon they put prisoners into when they take them off to jail. I suppose everybody thinks I'm being arrested."

She was sure that Mr. T. T. Tottingham thought so when she noticed his nose pressed against the glass of the doors and saw the great sighs he was heaving, as he replied to the questions the other people were asking him. She made a mental note to tell Mr. Tottingham about her balloon trip the first chance she had.

Officer Simpson introduced his colleague, described him as the fastest driver in the United Kingdom, and helped Miss Pickerell to climb up the very tall step into the automobile. She sat silently between the two policemen. She gritted her teeth when the car lurched forward. She clung to the edge of her seat when the driver, his feet holding the throttle wide open, accelerated his speed. The car zoomed past houses, lawns, trees, lakes. It screamed as they went around turns. And through the open window on the driver's side, the wind sounded like an unending gale.

"I must keep my cool," Miss Pickerell told herself. "That's what Euphus and Rosemary are always saying. If only I could!"

She closed her eyes when she could bear it no longer. She kept them shut tight until the driver brought the car to a shaking halt and Officer Simpson tapped her on the shoulder.

"All right, Miss Pickerell," he said. "Here's your balloon! And here's your pilot, Mr. Albert Angus Porridge!"

12
Across the Channel on a Flying Balloon

Miss Pickerell's heart sank right down to her shoes when she took a good look at the balloon. Even from a few feet away, she could see that the net covering the sphere-shaped gas bag was full of patches. Each patch came in a different size and color. Three especially large ones, bright orange like one of Euphus's favorite T-shirts, seemed definitely about to fall off.

"Mr. Porridge must have sewed them on himself," she observed to Officer Simpson, who was helping her to take the long jumping step out of the car. "And I'm sure he used basting stitches."

Officer Simpson made no comment. Miss Pickerell sighed. She gave the constable Mr. Farnier's telephone number, instructed him about calling, and walked over to inspect the basket in which she was going to travel.

"Mercy!" she whispered, when she saw that

it was not even as big as her hall wardrobe closet on Square Toe Farm. "And I can't imagine why it has a curtain hanging up on one side."

"I believe it is the rain curtain," Officer Simpson, who was listening, told her. "To protect people in the balloon, in case of a storm."

Miss Pickerell recalled only too vividly what the constable had said about thunderstorms and how they could set a hydrogen balloon on fire. For the life of her, she couldn't think how a rain curtain would help in such a situation. She decided not to speculate any further about this since this balloon used helium anyway. She began to look at the railing that ran like a picket fence around the basket. She had to take a very firm hold on herself when she noticed that some of the reeds which served as pickets were missing.

"Where's Mr. Porridge?" she asked, while she tried to push aside the picture of herself falling through one of the empty places. "I don't see Mr. Porridge."

"Yes, you do, Ma'am," a voice called up to her.

Mr. Porridge was sliding out from under the balloon. He had white wispy hair, watery blue eyes, and a very red nose. He sniffed loudly when he stood up.

"Mr. Albert Angus Porridge at your service, Ma'am," he said. "I was just making certain about the sticks. Until a balloon is ready to fly, it must be tied down proper to its sticks. The wind can blow it halfway 'round the world after it's filled with helium."

Officer Simpson nodded.

"This is Miss Pickerell," he said. "Your passenger to the French coast."

Mr. Porridge took a wad of chewing tobacco out of his coat pocket.

"You'll have a grand trip, Ma'am," he said, as he popped the tobacco into his mouth. "The wind's blowing fine. That's our propeller, you know, pushing us from behind to where we want to go. Now, about getting back?"

"I've arranged for that," Miss Pickerell told him. "We'll be picking up a package in Calais and returning on a Hovercraft. I'd like to do it all as fast as possible."

"We'll get started, then," Mr. Porridge said. "You go first into the basket, Ma'am. The Constable will untie the sticks for us."

Miss Pickerell took a brisk step forward. She stopped short almost immediately.

"What's that?" she asked, staring at the sandbags stacked up in the basket. "What are they for?"

"Ballast," Mr. Porridge replied. "To give us some weight."

"Weight?" Miss Pickerell questioned.

"Weight," Mr. Porridge repeated. "So that we can control our altitude."

"I thought you released the helium from the gas valve when you wanted to go down," Miss Pickerell said. "I read about that in—"

"Hold on! Hold on a bit, Ma'am!" Mr. Porridge interrupted. "There's the gas valve *and* the sandbags in my balloon."

"And when you want to go up," Miss Pickerell began, "I understand that you—"

"It helps when we throw some of the ballast off," Mr. Porridge said. "We throw and throw and . . ."

He nudged her forward as he talked, followed her into the basket, and grabbed the rope that held the balloon to the sticks below.

"Let 'er go!" he shouted to Officer Simpson.

The balloon gave a sudden jolt. Then it soared aloft, right up to the sky.

"That was a nice liftoff," Mr. Porridge commented, rolling up the rope and looking very pleased. "A real nice liftoff."

Miss Pickerell, wedged between Mr. Porridge and the sandbags, watched the launching field gradually grow indistinct as they flew higher

FOREVERMORE!
HM.M.M!
POLICE

and higher. They were almost up to the clouds now. Miss Pickerell wondered if she would be able to reach out and touch them. They looked so soft and fleecy, a little like the cotton candy that Rosemary always bought when she went to the county fair.

"Clouds can change just like *that*!" Mr. Porridge remarked, snapping his fingers to show Miss Pickerell exactly how. "But I doubt that we'll have a storm."

Miss Pickerell didn't think so, either. She stood looking down at the outlines of the towns and farms they were flying over and speculated about how long it would be before they got to Dover. The channel, she knew, was narrowest from Dover to Calais. But nobody had said anything about that.

"Mr. Porridge," she asked quickly, "we are flying to Dover, aren't we?"

"If that's what you want, Ma'am," Mr. Porridge replied.

"I do," Miss Pickerell told him.

Mr. Porridge chewed hard on his tobacco wad.

"We're headed in that general direction, is all I can truthfully say," he added. "In a balloon, we're at the mercy of nature."

"I beg your pardon?" Miss Pickerell asked.

"Ah, yes," Mr. Porridge sniffed, while he

took a fresh wad of tobacco out of his pocket. "We drift when the wind is calm. And we wait when it blows us fifty miles in the wrong direction."

"We don't wait at all," Miss Pickerell stated impatiently. "We go up and down so that we can adjust to the direction and intensity of the wind and keep moving in the direction that we want."

"You don't need to tell me about steering," Mr. Porridge said curtly. "And I don't hold with those newfangled notions about putting scientific steering devices in the balloons, either."

Miss Pickerell had a good mind to talk to him about some of the progress science was responsible for. She dismissed that idea when she noticed the change in the clouds. They had not gotten any darker. They seemed to have become much thicker, though. Everything in front of them was almost invisible.

"Best to get under those clouds," Mr. Porridge muttered, as he began pulling on the rope connected to the gas valve.

"Above them!" Miss Pickerell called out. "Above the clouds! The higher altitude will give us more speed."

"Either way," Mr. Porridge said. "I'll tell you when I see how the wind blows."

He did not have to make a decision, for the clouds broke up. They parted practically down the middle and the balloon flew between them, right out into the clear blue sky. Miss Pickerell breathed a sigh of relief and leaned back against the sandbags to relax. They were approaching open water now, she believed. She couldn't see the water yet but she thought she could make out the shapes of gorse and saxifrage and these, she knew, were seacoast flowers.

"It's all very comfortable at this moment," she remarked to Mr. Porridge.

Mr. Porridge grunted his agreement and searched in another pocket of his coat.

"You can sit down on the sandbags, if you like," he said. "You might want to do some of the knitting I suspect you have in your bag. Or you can watch me put this up."

He unfolded a large flag that he dragged out of his pocket.

"It's the tricolor flag of France," he said. "That's the country we're flying to. I like to show my respect."

He hummed the opening bars of the French national anthem as he tied the flag to the front of the basket.

"I picked that tune up in the Ducks and Drakes," he explained. "That's my local, my pub I should say, near Portobello Road. I live over a sweetshop, right around the corner. Five quid a week I pay, central heating included. Not bad for the money, but it gets a bit lonely. I'm not one to stay by myself too long. In the pub, I meet my chums. We . . . ."

He babbled on and on as the balloon gained altitude and moved swiftly forward. They were flying over the sea now. The waters looked rough and choppy. The wind was getting stronger, too, and the balloon was swaying back and forth. Miss Pickerell tightened the woolen scarf she had on around her hat and clung to the railing. Then, just as suddenly as it had started, the wind died down. The balloon changed its motion. It pitched and rocked and once, Miss Pickerell felt sure, it seemed nearly to spin around.

"What's happening?" she shouted.

"We're losing altitude," Mr. Porridge shouted back.

Miss Pickerell could see, as she leaned over the railing, how very rapidly they were going down. In a matter of minutes, maybe even seconds, they would be in the water.

"We'll never get up again, if we land down there," Mr. Porridge moaned. "With no wind to speak of, we'll never move again."

"The sandbags!" Miss Pickerell screamed. "The sandbags!"

"Not to panic!" Mr. Porridge replied, also screaming. "I'm getting to them."

Miss Pickerell did not wait. She lifted a bag and almost collapsed under its weight.

"Bend your knees!" Mr. Porridge said, still screaming. "Bend your knees when you pick up a heavy object."

One by one, Miss Pickerell picked up the sandbags and tossed them out on one side of the basket, while Mr. Porridge kept throwing them out on the other side. And gradually the balloon rose again, clearing the surface of the water and almost getting up to the clouds. Miss Pickerell sat down on the remaining sandbags and tried to catch her breath. Mr. Porridge sat down with her.

"There's nothing predictable about balloons," he said, sniffing again. "Not on a long journey, that is."

"It's not a *very* long journey," Miss Pickerell replied, while she consulted her watch. "By my calculations, we should be nearing Calais at about this time."

"Not when there's no land in sight," Mr. Porridge stated. "And there sure is none."

Miss Pickerell was inclined to disagree. She

believed she saw something ... something in the distance. But it was not until she remembered Mrs. Broadribb's second-best bird-watching glasses still lying in her knitting bag and peered through what seemed to her to be very extra-strong lenses that she felt more or less certain.

"Straight ahead!" she directed Mr. Porridge. "Straight ahead to those patches of green and brown soil!"

"Yes, Ma'am," Mr. Porridge grunted.

He kept bouncing the balloon up and down with the wind to shift it in the right direction, as Miss Pickerell went on watching and calling out her directions. They were getting closer and closer to land. She could see the coastline clearly now.

"We're practically ready to descend," she said, gratefully putting Mrs. Broadribb's glasses away and turning to look happily at Mr. Porridge.

Mr. Porridge appeared far from happy. His eyes were fixed gloomily on the valve at the top of the balloon and he was sniffing hard.

"We can't descend," he said hoarsely. "The valve's stuck. The valve that releases the helium to let us down."

Miss Pickerell started picking up sandbags

again. She changed her mind when she realized what she was doing.

"I must pull myself together," she told herself. "We want to go *down* now, not *up.*"

She turned resolutely to Mr. Porridge.

"What should I do?" she asked. "What should I do, Mr. Porridge?"

Mr. Porridge only shook his head.

"It's stuck bad," he muttered as he kept staring desperately at the valve. "Stuck real bad!"

"Then we'll just have to *fix* it," Miss Pickerell told him. "How do we go about it?"

"We have to break the hose connection," Mr. Porridge replied, "the one that releases the helium. It's a long, hard pull."

Miss Pickerell stood behind Mr. Porridge to help him pull. She did not pause when she felt her legs beginning to cave in under her. She drew them up and pulled again.

She and Mr. Porridge were both fighting for breath and Mr. Porridge was mumbling, "We'll be up here until we crash into the shores of France," when the valve came loose. The helium began to pour out in gusts and the balloon went straight down. Miss Pickerell, too frightened and exhausted even to ask whether this was going to be like a parachute landing, flopped over the front of the basket. She was unconscious when they touched the ground.

13
"I'll Go Down Fighting"

Miss Pickerell did not fully regain consciousness until she was halfway back to England aboard *La Belle Matilde.* That was the name of the Hovercraft. She learned it from Mr. Porridge, who was sitting beside her in a deck chair when she opened her eyes.

"You went into a dead faint, Ma'am," he told her. "The Customs man fetched you some smelling salts and got you out of it, but then you went off again. More like a sleep though, that was. I told them not to wake you when they carried you onto the ship. Nice and smooth, she rides, just like a regular ship."

Miss Pickerell, raising herself up a little to watch the gliding progress across the water, nodded.

"*Matilde*'s her name," Mr. Porridge went on, "*La Belle Matilde.* The captain says that's the same as our beautiful Mathilda. Named her after his sweetheart, the owner did, I expect."

"After his cat," Miss Pickerell said weakly. "Where . . . where is the owner?"

"He couldn't come," Mr. Porridge replied. "It was the captain and his helper who settled you nice and cozy in the chair with the wool blanket over you. And they brought my balloon up, stacked ever so neat onto a wheelbarrow that they're giving me the loan of. The captain said he was the owner's father. I couldn't rightly make out who the helper was. They don't speak a whole lot of English, neither one of them does. Now, the Customs man, and the lady who was waiting, they speak it good and proper. I mentioned that to both of them."

Miss Pickerell was suddenly alert.

"My package!" she shouted, as she kicked away the blanket and staggered to her feet. "The package that Mr. Farnier—"

"I'm taking good care of it for you," Mr. Porridge assured her. "You can be certain of that. I'm not one to lose things, I said to the lady when she gave it to me. It's more like two packages than one, though, if you count the teakettle."

He walked across the deck to a lifeboat, stooped way down, and picked up a long flat parcel, wrapped in brown paper and tied around with a string. Then he leaned over still farther and brought up a covered iron kettle with a brown wooden handle attached to both sides at the top.

"There's about what you Americans call half a gallon in here for sure," he remarked, as he settled the kettle next to Miss Pickerell's chair.

"I'll look at the package first," Miss Pickerell told him. "That's Mr. Farnier's manuscript."

Mr. Porridge helped her untie the string. The manuscript was very thick and bound between hard covers, like a book. Miss Pickerell turned to the introduction, on the page under Mr. Farnier's name and address.

"Ethanol," Mr. Farnier had written, "can be obtained by the fermentation of sugars from wheat and other grains. The starches and complex grain sugars are changed to a simple sugar such as glucose by enzyme action. The glucose is then fermented into alcohol."

She paused to apologize to Mr. Porridge.

"It's secret," she explained, "or I'd read it aloud to you. But this part is almost exactly what Euphus told me."

"Euphus?" Mr. Porridge asked, looking blank.

"My middle nephew," Miss Pickerell said, as she returned to the manuscript.

"The fermentation of many agricultural products," she read, "and of inedible plants such as weeds and of ordinary garbage can be speeded up with the powerful enzyme that I have developed by uniting the genes of different bacterial strains (details on page 41)."

Miss Pickerell nearly jumped out of the deck chair in her excitement.

"This is wonderful!" she exclaimed. "I'm sure Parliament will agree."

Mr. Porridge sniffed loudly.

"I don't rightly know what you're talking about, Miss, since it's such a secret," he said, "but I wouldn't count on Parliament approving anything so lightly. Our British Parliament is a most cautious body. And to my way of thinking, that's the way it should be."

Miss Pickerell barely listened. She turned from the introduction to the summary at the beginning of Mr. Farnier's article:

Procedure

1. Crush the waste vegetation or garbage.
2. Place it in a large rotating stainless steel vat kept at a temperature of 38 degrees Celsius.
3. Add Bacteria Culture X99.
4. As fermentation occurs, allow alcohol to drain out of hole on bottom of vat.
5. Evaporate the alcohol in a container and condense it to make almost pure alcohol.
6. Use the bacteria that have multiplied in the vat to start new vats.
7. The process produces both alcohol and additional bacteria to make more alcohol with a minimum of time and cost.

Miss Pickerell smiled as she closed the book, put it back in the brown wrapping paper, and looked up at Mr. Porridge again.

"I'm taking the manuscript and the contents of the kettle to the House of Commons," she explained. "I'm going there the minute that we get off this Hovercraft. I'll walk right over!"

"Not from the Tower Pier, you won't," Mr. Porridge stated.

"The Tower Pier?" Miss Pickerell questioned.

"That's where we land," Mr. Porridge told her. "We go that way because the Tower Bridge can lift itself up to let a ship like this pass through. You'd best take the water-bus to Westminster Pier. I'm going in that direction, myself. I had it in mind to drop in on . . ."

Miss Pickerell was not listening. The ship was slowing down. She could feel the change in the motion and though she was not sure, she believed she heard the blowing of a warning whistle. She knew it for a fact when she saw the captain and his assistant, both dressed in white linen uniforms with gold badges, and blue caps on their heads, approach her. The one she thought might be the father of the owner picked up her knitting bag and umbrella. The other man carried the wrapped-up manuscript and the kettle of ethanol. Mr. Porridge, pushing the wheelbarrow, walked behind them. The captain politely escorted Miss Pickerell off the ship. He and his assistant raced with her and Mr. Porridge to the waiting water-bus.

"I'll get the tickets," Mr. Porridge told her. "You'd best see if you can find a seat."

There were none. The water-bus was crowded with people who seemed to be returning from work. Most of the men carried rolled-up umbrellas and the morning newspaper. One of them rose to give Miss Pickerell his seat.

"I'm getting off at the next stop, anyway," he said, when she thanked him.

Miss Pickerell highly approved of the water-bus as a means of reducing traffic on a city's streets and highways. She made a mental note to be sure to remember to tell the Governor about it. She was repeating this note to herself when the boat stopped at the Westminster Pier and she and Mr. Porridge got off.

"Mercy!" she exclaimed. "Parliament is right here. I can just run in."

"Are you sure you can manage?" anxiously asked Mr. Porridge, who was panting behind his wheelbarrow. "That kettle is heavy."

Miss Pickerell did not think this was anything to be concerned about. She had such a short way to walk. She went right up to the door of the House of Commons after she said goodbye to Mr. Porridge.

The door was closed. Miss Pickerell put the kettle of ethanol down and knocked politely. There was no answer. She knocked more loudly, but still no one answered. She decided to forget about her manners and leaned against the door to *push* it open. It did not budge. It was shut, shut tight.

"Oh, no!" Miss Pickerell breathed. "It can't be! It simply can't!!"

But the door remained shut when she continued to knock on it. And nobody came when she called out, "Yoo-hoo! Please let me in!"

She raced up and down the Square looking for another door that might be open. She couldn't find one anywhere.

The tower clock, the one that the taxi driver had called Big Ben, rang out the hour. Miss Pickerell counted the chimes. She also checked with her watch. It was seven o'clock.

"They've probably all gone home," she whispered, as she stared at the darkened windows. "I'll have to come back tomorrow."

She picked up the kettle of ethanol and looked around for a place to sit down.

"I'm tired," she said to herself. "And I'm restless. I'd like to get this thing over with."

One of the statues nearby, she noticed, had a large base at the bottom. She settled herself and her packages there.

"It's because I'm so worried that I can't bear waiting," she said, unhappily remembering what Mr. Porridge had said about how very cautious Parliament was. "I don't *want* to make another speech, but I *will,* if I have to. I'm not walking out on those poor animals."

She wondered what questions the Speaker and the members of the House of Commons would ask her about the ethanol. She decided to study the summary in the manuscript and to memorize every word in it before she went to bed.

"I'll answer their questions!" she said, talking out loud this time. "I'll fight for the ethanol. And if I can't answer, I'll go down fighting. What's more, I'll get right up again!!"

14
Thank You, Euphus

From where she sat, facing in the direction opposite the river, Miss Pickerell could see the way Parliament Square led into a park and how the streets went uphill from the river toward the part of London where her hotel was located. She could also see the taxis, full to bursting, that were still riding the streets and the bicycles that weaved their way in and out of the traffic. It seemed to her that half of London had calmly transferred itself to bicycles and that the other half was squeezing itself into a shared taxi.

"Well, I'll just have to go and squeeze myself into one of them, too," she decided, as she wearily dragged herself up from her cold stone seat. "I'll try the street near the park. Most of the taxis seem to be passing along there."

Inside the park, there was not even a hint of the troubles that had descended on London. The grass looked like a green carpet. The flowers were beautiful enough to be in a county competition. And at the edge of a lake, a lady with a big white shopping bag was handing out bread to geese that stood waiting in front of her. Miss Pickerell wondered why she had not fed them earlier in the day and then decided that she probably had and was giving them another snack now. The geese looked very well cared for.

"I wish I could think that the animals at the Home for Retired and Disabled Animals would always have something to eat, too," she said, as she let out a deep sigh. "I wish . . . Oh, what's the use of just wishing?"

She moved toward the street where she had seen the taxicabs. There were none passing now. A few buses went by, but she had no idea as to where they were going or even where they stopped to pick up passengers. She kept on walking. She walked and walked with her knitting bag and umbrella hanging over her left arm, Mr. Farnier's thick manuscript cradled in the crook of that arm, and the wooden handle of the ethanol kettle clutched in her right hand.

"I'm not even sure that I'm walking in the correct direction," she murmured, as she paused for breath. "Of course, I'm going away from the river, but that's not enough. I'd better ask someone."

There were not very many people she could ask, though. Some seemed to be in such a hurry, she did not have the heart to delay them. Two young men whom she did ask said they were strangers in town themselves. One suggested that she might inquire in the greengrocer's shop across the way. But that shop and also the drapery shop next door were closed, Miss Pickerell found, when she tried them. The only place that was open seemed to be what Mr. Porridge had called a pub at the end of the street. A sign on the window announced that it was The Pig and Whistle. Miss Pickerell could smell the beer when she entered.

"I'd like some information," she said to the stout, red-faced woman who was standing behind the bar, busily filling up glasses for the crowd of men in front of it. "I'm an American and I'm lost and . . ."

"And you look beat for sure," the woman said, handing the bottle she was holding to another barmaid and joining Miss Pickerell. "Come and sit down, love, and let me get you a pot of coffee."

She led Miss Pickerell to the back of the room and settled her at a table with a blue and white checked cloth on it. Two women and a man sat at an adjoining table. Two other men, at the far end of the room, were quietly playing a game of darts.

"Now, will it be coffee or a shandy like the people at the next table are having?" the woman asked Miss Pickerell. "I can mix you up a nice shandy, half beer and half ginger ale or half beer and half lemonade."

"Coffee," Miss Pickerell said. "Strong, black coffee."

"That's what Americans like, isn't it?" the woman laughed. "A good cup of coffee."

She came back with the coffee and a plate full of buns and sat down beside Miss Pickerell.

"Lost, are you?" she said. "Well, we'll soon get that sorted out. Where are you staying, love?"

She whistled when Miss Pickerell told her the name of the hotel.

"That's a good long way from here," she said. "I don't expect you can find a taxi. There's the underground, but that will be jammed. And you'll still have to walk at the other end. Now, you could take a bus from Westminster, a number three, or maybe an eleven or a twelve. I'm not positive, myself, and you'd likely get lost again. Wait, wait half a moment!"

She marched over to the bar and returned

almost immediately, accompanied by a man with a cloth cap and a ragged moustache.

"This here's Harry," she said. "He works for the railroad. In the lost-property office. He knows all about getting around this city."

Harry gulped. He said nothing. He simply stared at Miss Pickerell. Then he took off his cap.

"You're . . . you're Miss Pickerell!" he whispered. "I've seen your picture in the papers. And there's a colored photo of you in the advertising poster over the bar."

He turned impatiently to the barmaid.

"What's the matter with you, Marge?" he asked. "Haven't you got eyes in your head to recognize Miss Pickerell?"

"Never you mind the eyes in my head," Marge retorted. "Miss Pickerell's in trouble. She has no transport to get her back to her hotel."

Harry pulled on his moustache and looked thoughtful.

"Well, there's the goods train running at this hour," he said. "It carries freight and runs on coal and belches smoke, but it's not a bit crowded and—"

"Don't talk nonsense, Harry," Marge interrupted. "The goods train doesn't go anywhere near Knightsbridge."

"You never said a word about Knightsbridge," Harry argued.

Miss Pickerell smiled. She was feeling much better. She had poured herself two cups of coffee from the pot and eaten some of the buns on the plate. She thought she might be able to go on with her walk now.

"I wish I knew somebody with a car," Harry commented when she mentioned this. "*And* with some petrol in it. Myself, I get around on a bike. Always have and . . ."

He paused while he looked doubtfully first at Miss Pickerell and then at her knitting bag, her umbrella, her wrapped-up package, and at the very large teakettle.

"It's a long way to walk," he said.

"It certainly is," Marge agreed.

"Now, if a lady like you, Miss Pickerell," he went on hesitantly, "wouldn't mind riding with me on my bicycle, I could stand up to pedal and you could have the seat in back of me and—"

Miss Pickerell did not even let him finish his sentence.

"When can we start?" she asked.

"Whenever you want," Harry told her. "My bicycle's outside."

Marge wrapped the ethanol kettle around with three bar towels and stood it up carefully, next to the manuscript in the bicycle basket. She put the knitting bag on top for extra protection against jiggling. She also helped Miss Pickerell button her sweater and retie her scarf.

"I'll be seeing you at the parade," she told Miss Pickerell. "Harry and I are planning to buy window seats. All the people with houses along the route are selling them."

"Don't do that," Miss Pickerell shouted, as Harry pushed off. "I'll find tickets for you."

Harry pedaled for a few feet and then asked her if she wanted him to point out some of the sights. He did not wait for her to answer.

"Down there on the other side of the park," he began, "is Number Ten Downing Street. That's where our Prime Minister lives. Very

nice, all our Prime Ministers have been, very eager to do what's right for the country. This one's having a hard time, trying to manage things a bit different. Being at the top is not always easy."

Miss Pickerell looked back to Ten Downing Street. She caught only a glimpse of a wall at the end of the park.

"And right next to Parliament," Harry continued, "is our Westminster Abbey. That's where our Royalty gets crowned, all fancy like."

Miss Pickerell remembered the pictures of Westminster Abbey she had seen from time to time in the newspapers. On special occasions, the pictures showed the Queen riding in the royal coach, behind the team of horses that was taking her to Westminster Abbey.

"We're coming to Buckingham Palace now," Harry went on. "Our Queen resides in Buckingham Palace."

Miss Pickerell gazed behind the gates at the long building with what looked like a thousand windows. They were all dark. She didn't believe the Queen was at home.

Harry talked and talked. He talked about the polished brass knobs that he called knockers on the doors of the houses that they passed and about the black-painted iron railings in front of the houses and about how the flowers in the window boxes shone in the light of the street lamps that were being turned on. Miss Pickerell wished he would stop. Something was stirring around in the back of her head, something important, something she wanted to do. Harry came into it somewhere. And Euphus. And Mr. Farnier. And her recipe for peppermintade . . .

She was still trying to figure out what it was when Harry left her at the hotel and bicycled off, calling, "Toodle-oo, Miss Pickerell!" It wasn't until after she went into the garden shed to make sure about Nancy Agatha and saw the printed sheet that Euphus had brought back from the pizza factory spread out under the full milk pail that everything came back to her.

"Forevermore!" she exclaimed, while she stared at the picture of the Prime Minister in the middle of the page. The Prime Minister was eating a slice of pizza and congratulating the owner of the pizza factory on his pioneering efforts in establishing a new industry in England. The exact words of the Prime Minister were printed below the picture, right above the name and address of the pizza factory.

Miss Pickerell remembered very distinctly now about her new peppermintade recipe and what Professor Humwhistel had said when Mrs. Broadribb had turned her nose up at it. "The life of the pioneer is usually a difficult one," he had told her. "Even in the matter of recipes." And Euphus, who had probably been listening, had repeated it to Mr. Farnier. And Mr. Farnier, who no doubt had the same problems, had said it back to her. And Harry had said practically the same thing about the Prime Minister.

"Thank you, Euphus," Miss Pickerell whispered, as she patted her cow's head and decided that she definitely did not have to endure the agony of waiting until tomorrow. "Thank you, Euphus, for bringing back the picture. I *know* what I have to do *now*. *I'm* going to the *top!!*"

15
Ten Downing Street

Miss Pickerell did not waste even a minute in carrying out her plan. She asked the doorman immediately to have her automobile brought out from the hotel garage.

"Half a gallon of gas should get me down to the river and back, I believe," she said to him.

"With a bit to spare, I should think, Miss," he informed her. "If you can perhaps tell me just where you're going, I may be in a better position to advise you."

"To Number Ten Downing Street," Miss Pickerell replied promptly. "That's where your Prime Minister lives, I have been told. I understand that this Prime Minister has a very pioneering spirit."

The doorman gulped.

"I . . . I expect so, Miss," he said. "I have never had the occasion to meet the Prime Minister."

"Well, I have never met our United States

President, either," Miss Pickerell admitted. "But I would have no hesitation in visiting him, if I could tell him about something that's good for the country."

The doorman did not answer. He helped Miss Pickerell into her automobile, asked the attendant to fetch her cow when Miss Pickerell said that Nancy Agatha deserved a ride after all she'd been through, and watched silently when Euphus raced up the driveway and jumped into the trailer with the cow.

"Is it true that you took a balloon trip to get the ethanol-making process?" he asked instantly. "Why didn't you take me? I know a lot about balloons."

In the very next breath he gave Miss Pickerell a short history of ballooning and told her that he and the Governor had been to a waxworks museum, eaten fish and chips from a man who sold them on the street, and visited Hyde Park Corner where, the Governor said, anybody could get up and make a speech.

"Only there was nobody speaking when we got there," he added. "The Governor was very disappointed. He said he'd wait another ten minutes. I left. Where are you going, Aunt Lavinia?"

"To give the ethanol and the method for making it to the Prime Minister," Miss Pickerell replied, turning away from her inspection of how Nancy Agatha was getting along in the trailer and proceeding to give her full attention to stacking the kettle and the manuscript carefully at her feet. "To explain to the Prime Minister why ethanol should be put into cars as fuel."

"Super!" Euphus shouted. "I can explain the science part. The Prime Minister is going to ask questions about the science part."

Miss Pickerell nodded as she steered the automobile and the trailer out of the driveway. She wished she were looking somewhat more presentable for this visit to the Prime Minister. She untied her scarf and put it into her knitting bag at the next traffic light. She was able to smooth out her skirt and wipe her glasses and to tuck a few of her hairpins into place when another traffic light took longer to change. She was pleased to see that Euphus appeared very neat and clean.

Number Ten Downing Street was a little difficult for her to find. It was one of a row of identical four-story brick houses and Miss Pickerell kept missing it until she saw the street lamp over the entrance and could make out the number. The door was opened by a gentleman who blinked when he saw Nancy Agatha in her trailer and the kettle in Miss Pickerell's hand.

But he bowed politely when Miss Pickerell introduced Euphus and herself and explained her errand.

"The Prime Minister is at a meeting," he said. "I am one of the Secretaries. I will be glad to transmit both the manuscript and the ethanol, however. I can also assure you that the Prime Minister has heard all about your recommendations to Parliament and will do everything possible to help. Would you like to come in for a moment, Miss Pickerell?"

Miss Pickerell thought she would rather not because she wanted to keep an eye on her cow.

"But I can tell you everything right here," she added. "The procedure for preparing the ethanol is in the manuscript. The ethanol sample is in the tea kettle. I brought a lot for the Speaker to test out."

The Secretary nodded solemnly.

"Ethanol is a very practical solution," Miss Pickerell went on. "Oil and gas and coal can be used up. But farmers can always grow another year's supply of corn or grain or—"

"My biology teacher says," Euphus interrupted, "that you can also use sugar-cane stalks and grapefruit husks and wood chips and—"

"And garbage," Miss Pickerell added, "and other wastes that are readily available."

"I think that using ethanol is really using solar energy," Euphus commented. "The sun is what helps the agricultural products to grow."

"Yes," Miss Pickerell agreed. "It's a way of *growing fuel.* Be sure to tell that to the Prime Minister."

"Be sure to tell about that study, too," Euphus exclaimed, "the study that showed how ethanol can improve mileage. *At least* five percent more per gallon."

The Secretary smiled.

"It seems very reasonable, indeed," he said, "and I will be sure to give all the information to the Prime Minister. I'll hope to see you at the parade, Miss Pickerell."

Miss Pickerell wished she could feel more confident about the prospect. She said as much to Euphus on the way back to the hotel.

"Maybe it's because I'm so tired," she commented. "I'll go to bed as soon as I put Nancy Agatha into her shed and call Mr. Kettelson."

She told Euphus to go to bed, too, when he followed her up to her room.

"It's only nine o'clock," he objected. "I want to hear what Mr. Kettelson has to say."

When he answered the telephone, Mr. Kettelson spent a little time talking about his business and about how he was planning to discharge his assistant. But he proceeded quickly to the subject of Pumpkins and Euphus's six sisters and brothers who were now staying on the farm.

"Rosemary's the only one who presents a problem," he told Miss Pickerell. "She wants Pumpkins to stay on her bed at night. He prefers not to."

Euphus sighed when she hung up.

"You never let me talk to him," he complained. "But it doesn't matter. One of us had better call Scotland Yard now."

Miss Pickerell threw him a severely questioning look as she proceeded to take her valise out of the closet and to go on with the unpacking she had never finished.

"We'll have to tell them about the Governor," Euphus insisted. "He's still not here and he said he'd be back in ten minutes. We'll need to give all his vital statistics. Scotland Yard always wants full details about age, height, weight, and birthmarks—especially birthmarks."

"Nonsense!" Miss Pickerell told him.

But she did feel more than a little worried about the Governor. He had assured Euphus about the ten minutes *before* she and Euphus started out to see the Prime Minister. That was nearly two hours ago. All *sorts* of terrible things could have happened to him!

Miss Pickerell was trying very hard to put a particularly gruesome possibility out of her mind when the steady knocking on the door began. Her heart practically skipped a beat. Euphus raced to open the door. Mr. Cyril Chuff-Cooper entered.

"Mercy!" Miss Pickerell whispered, as she stared at him.

His thinning red hair stood straight up on his head. The short hairs on his upper lip, where he must have forgotten to shave, seemed all stiff and about to sprout out in all directions. And his eyes were almost popping out of his face.

"The Governor!" Miss Pickerell gasped.

"He's on his way up," Mr. Chuff-Cooper replied. "He's talking to the reporters."

"The reporters!" Miss Pickerell breathed. "There's been an accident! Or an argument with one of those Hyde Park speakers!"

Mr. Cyril Chuff-Cooper's eyes seemed to grow even larger as he stared at her.

"Haven't you heard, Miss Pickerell?" he asked, almost screaming with excitement. "Hasn't anyone told you about the parade?"

"The news has just broken," the Governor, walking into the room with a swarm of reporters in front of him, shouted over their heads. "Automobile fuel rations have been removed."

Miss Pickerell sat down on the edge of the nearest chair.

"Impossible!" she proclaimed. "They couldn't have tested the ethanol yet. They didn't have time."

"They *did,*" a woman reporter with an especially huge camera told her. "It's a fast-acting enzyme and takes only a few minutes, I understand. The Prime Minister called up some top scientists to do the testing."

"The Prime Minister has a way of coming right to the point on such issues," a man reporter with another camera added.

"You can go ahead with your interviews and pictures now, ladies and gentlemen," Mr. Cyril Chuff-Cooper called out.

"Wait!" Euphus shouted from where he was lying on the floor, switching the television set to channels one, two, and three and back again. "Wait for me!"

He turned the volume up before he got to his feet. The news came blaring out:

> Fuel rations have been removed. The International Antique Car Fair, which had been indefinitely postponed, is now scheduled to start at 10 A.M. tomorrow. Car owners are delighted with the news about the removal of gasoline rations. And all Londoners, as well as Britishers to the south, are looking forward to watching the parade, which will be headed by Miss Pickerell, the lady who flew across the channel in a balloon to provide us with the ethanol sample and the procedure for the ethanol tests. Mr. Henri Farnier, the French scientist who developed the ethanol to take the place of gasoline in motor cars, has been notified. He will be honored next week in a special ceremony in . . .

Miss Pickerell was feeling so relieved that she hardly noticed the number of pictures the reporters were taking. And she did not even object when the Governor posed her between himself and Euphus for still another picture. But she refused to answer the questions the reporters asked her.

"Euphus and the Governor can tell you everything," she told them. "I . . . I'm hungry."

She ate the supper that Room Service brought up, while Euphus and the Governor were talking to the reporters. She started getting ready for bed as soon as they all left. Mr. Cyril Chuff-Cooper returned to give her one last message.

"Don't forget the hat!" he called from the other side of the door. "Don't forget to wear the hat!"

"Don't forget to send Mr. Albert Angus Porridge his check for the cross-channel balloon ride," Miss Pickerell retorted. "You can get the address and the bill from Officer Simpson at the Metropolitan Police."

"Oh, no!" Mr. Chuff-Cooper exclaimed.

"Oh, yes!" Miss Pickerell told him.

She began running the water into the bathtub as soon as she heard his retreating footsteps. It was a pale pink bathtub, she noticed. It matched very nicely the color of the rug and the wallpaper in the other room.

16
An Invitation from the Queen

The morning of the parade dawned bright and clear. Miss Pickerell got up very early to make her preparations. She packed her knitting bag and proceeded to the matter of dressing herself properly. She took particular pains with the way she put on her hat.

"I'm going to *earn* my money," she declared, as she jabbed two long hatpins into the felt to make sure the hat would *stay* straight on her head. "If that's what Mr. Anthony Piffle is paying me for, that's what he'll have."

She met Mr. Cyril Chuff-Cooper when she was crossing the lobby to the hotel dining room. He looked her over critically.

"Splendid!" he said at last. "Precisely the effect we want!"

They walked together into the dining room.

"I was just coming up to show you the morning newspapers," Mr. Chuff-Cooper went on, as he settled himself in the chair opposite Miss Pickerell and spread the papers out on the table. "Your picture is in all of them. More will be taken on the line of march. There will be more stories, as well. I plan to write a few of the press releases to hand on to the papers, myself. Mine will be more dramatic."

Miss Pickerell concentrated on her tea and toast and changed the subject.

"I want two tickets for the parade," she said. "For some very special friends of mine. I would like them in the reviewing stand."

"We don't have a reviewing stand," Mr. Chuff-Cooper replied. "We don't need one. All the important people are parading with us. The Lord Mayor of London has promised to wear his robes and chain and—"

"Then I will take two window-seat tickets," Miss Pickerell interrupted. "In the front, please."

"I have absolutely nothing to do with those window-seat sales," Mr. Chuff-Cooper said, shuddering. "Who are these special friends of yours?"

"Marge and Harry, at The Pig and Whistle," Miss Pickerell said.

"The Pig and Whistle?" Mr. Cyril Chuff-Cooper repeated.

"Yes," Miss Pickerell told him. "Marge is the

chief barmaid. Harry works for the railroad."

Mr. Cyril Chuff-Cooper opened his mouth, closed it, and opened it again.

"Bless you, Miss Pickerell!" he whispered.

Miss Pickerell stared. Mr. Cyril Chuff-Cooper stared too, but not at her. He seemed to be lost in a vision of his own.

"Miss Pickerell," he exclaimed, as he jumped out of his chair. "You have just given me the story of the year. The British public will love it—Marge and Harry standing in the trailer with Nancy Agatha and . . . No, I'm putting Euphus and the Governor there. I'll have Marge and Harry sit up front with you. That will do it. The Pig and Whistle, you said?"

He was out of the dining room before Miss Pickerell could say another word. She sighed and went to see Nancy Agatha.

"You'd better have a hearty breakfast," she told the cow, while she led her toward the thick grass under the green apple tree. "You'll be going for a ride soon. I'm just stepping upstairs now for my knitting bag and umbrella. Then I'll come back and get you."

The telephone rang as soon as she entered her room. It was Mr. Anthony Piffle calling long-distance. He had set his alarm for 3:00 A.M., he explained, so that he could reach her before the parade started and wish her luck.

The Governor knocked on the door a few minutes later to ask if he might escort her down. He was now wearing a pair of pearl-buttoned gloves, Miss Pickerell noticed, and a white carnation in his lapel.

Everybody in the lobby except Mr. T. T. Tottingham cheered when Miss Pickerell and the Governor walked through. The automobile and the trailer were standing outside the revolving doors. A garage man was leaning over the car and pouring gasoline into the tank.

"I attended to that, Miss," the doorman told her. "I also took the liberty of suggesting to your nephew that he might bring the cow out, seeing as how you would be all dressed up and such."

Nancy Agatha and Mr. Cyril Chuff-Cooper, with Marge and Harry crammed into the small car beside him, arrived in front of the hotel at about the same time. Marge had squeezed her stout figure into a bright summer suit. Harry's hair was wet and neatly brushed back from a very straight center part. Mr. Chuff-Cooper transferred them into Miss Pickerell's automobile.

"Coo!" Marge exclaimed, stopping to kiss Miss Pickerell. "This is lovely! Thanks ever so!!"

Harry said nothing. He was watching the

fife-and-drum corps now standing ready in front of Mr. Cyril Chuff-Cooper's car. Miss Pickerell did not pay much attention to the band. She had just noticed the constable in the park across the street.

"Officer Simpson!" she shouted, waving for him to join her. "Officer Simpson!"

Both the Constable and Mr. Cyril Chuff-Cooper looked a little dismayed when Miss Pickerell insisted that Officer Simpson must have a place of honor in the parade. The Constable said that he couldn't walk off his job without permission. Miss Pickerell said that Mr. Chuff-Cooper could arrange all that. Mr. Chuff-Cooper sighed and went to talk to the Lord Mayor. He was sitting in the limousine right behind the trailer. Miss Pickerell recognized him because of his robe and chain. The other dignitaries in the cars behind him were wearing striped trousers and tailcoats.

"All set!" Mr. Cyril Chuff-Cooper shouted when he returned. "Into position, everybody!"

Nancy Agatha, Euphus, and the Governor were already in the trailer. They stood, one on each side of the cow. Mr. Chuff-Cooper placed Constable Simpson in back of the cow. He stood with his helmet on, towering over her. Miss Pickerell thought they made a very handsome picture. She smiled when she stepped into her automobile.

The streets were lined with people. She could see some of them across the police roadblock that kept them from getting too close to the hotel. They laughed and cheered and gave out a great shout when Mr. Cyril Chuff-Cooper called, "Off we go!" from his car up front, and the fife-and-drum corps began playing "God Save the Queen."

People were everywhere, Miss Pickerell saw, as she drove along—in the windows, lifting their babies up for a better look, on the street corners, selling glasses of lemonade, at tables and chairs set out on lawns. They applauded and screamed her name when she passed. Marge waved to them. Harry just muttered.

"Blimey!" he burst out finally. "That Mr. Chuff-Cooper chap is daft in the head. He's supposed to go down Constitution Hill, past Buckingham Palace, and across the Victoria Bridge, if he wants to get to Sussex Downs. Take a look at where he's leading us instead."

"He's not daft," Marge told him. "He's taking us around to show Miss Pickerell off. And look, Harry, look at those antique automobiles joining the parade. That's a 1907 Garford-Studebaker! And a Maxwell and a Stutz Bearcat. And there's a White Steamer."

Harry snorted and began telling Miss Pickerell the names of the places that they passed. He named Oxford Circus and Piccadilly and Trafalgar Square and Russell Square and Kensington Park and Hampton Court and . . . Miss Pickerell couldn't see any of them. The flashbulbs kept popping into her face and blinding her eyes.

At the corner of what Harry said was Wellington Crescent and where Marge pointed out the statue of the Duke of Wellington sitting high on his stone horse, Mr. Chuff-Cooper suddenly halted. A young man, dressed in the uni-

form of the Royal Air Force, was signaling to him from a long elegant limousine. The young man drove straight past him and on to Miss Pickerell. He got out of the car, stood up very erect, and handed her a note.

"A message from the Queen!" Mr. Cyril Chuff-Cooper shouted. "A message from the Queen!"

More shouts came from Euphus and the Governor and Officer Simpson and from the Lord Mayor and the people on the streets.

"Read it aloud!" they called. "Read it aloud!"

The television mikes moved up close to catch every word. The crowds stood hushed as she read:

> Miss Lavinia Pickerell:
>
> The Queen is most grateful for the help you wished to extend to her country in its recent time of crisis and requests your presence for tea in the Royal Chambers at 4 P.M. on Tuesday next.
>
> Press Officer
> Buckingham Palace

"Speech! Speech!" the crowd roared.

Miss Pickerell braced herself. She stood up in the automobile and leaned over toward the microphones.

"It's Euphus," she said, after a deep breath, "my middle nephew, Euphus, who knew about the ethanol. And it's the Governor, the Governor of my state, who wanted to do all he could for international cooperation. And it's Mr. Farnier, the friend of Euphus's biology teacher, who discovered the new ethanol-making procedure."

Euphus waved. The Governor bowed. The crowd cheered. "Hip, hip, hooray, Mr. Farnier!!"

"I'm going home after this parade," Miss Pickerell went on, "to Square Toe County,

where I live on a farm with my cow, Nancy Agatha, and my cat, Pumpkins, and where we have a wonderful Home for Retired and Disabled Animals. You must all come and see it sometime. I will be glad to show you around."

The crowd kept on cheering. Miss Pickerell sat down and leaned back in the automobile. Marge kissed her again.

"What are you going to wear, Ducks?" she asked. "To go and visit the Queen?"

Miss Pickerell was not concerned about that. She was wondering whether the Queen, who loved dogs and horses so much, might perhaps be interested in meeting her cow.

About the Authors

ELLEN MACGREGOR created the character of Miss Pickerell in the early 1950's. With a little help from Miss MacGregor, Lavinia Pickerell had four remarkable adventures. Then, in 1954, Ellen MacGregor died. And it was not until 1964, after a long, long search, that Miss P. finally found Dora Pantell.

DORA PANTELL says that she has been writing something at some time practically since she was born. Among the "somethings" are scripts for radio and television, magazine stories, newspaper articles, books for all ages, and, of course, the Miss Pickerell adventures, which, she insists, she enjoys best of all. As good places for writing, she suggests airplanes, dentists' waiting rooms, and a semi-dark theater when the play gets dull. Ms. Pantell spends a good deal of the rest of her time reading non-violent detective stories, listening to classical music on Station WNCN, and watching the television shows on Channel 13, in New York City. But mostly she is busy keeping the peace among her three cats, Haiku Darling, Eliza Doolittle, and the newest addition, the incorrigible Cluny Brown.

About the Artist

CHARLES GEER has been illustrating for as long as he can remember and has more books to his credit than he can count. He has recently moved to a rambling old house on the Chesapeake, on Maryland's Eastern Shore. When he is not bent over the drawing board or the typewriter—Mr. Geer has written as well as illustrated two middle-group books—he is at work on the twenty-two foot sailboat he built himself, or taking long backpack hikes, or sailing.